Blazer Drive

LIGHTNING ON ICE SERIES

SERIES

Blazer Drive

SIGMUND BROUWER

WORD PUBLISHING
Dallas•London•Vancouver•Melbourne

To Teagan James—
We all look forward to
seeing you on skates.

BLAZER DRIVE

Managing Editor: Laura Minchew
Project Editor: Beverly Phillips

Library of Congress Cataloging–in–Publication Data

Brouwer, Sigmund, 1959–
    Blazer drive.
        p. cm.—(Lightning on ice series ; 5)
    "Word kids!"
    Summary: With playoffs ahead and a chance to play a few games
in the National Hockey League, Josh hesitates to get involved when
he finds more than a dozen dead cattle on his dad's ranch.
    ISBN 0–8499–3983–6
    [1. Hockey—Fiction. 2. Ranch Life—Fiction. 3. Mystery and
detective stories.] I. Title. II. Series: Brouwer, Sigmund, 1959–
Lightning on ice series ; 5.
PZ7.B79984Br 1996
[Fic]—DC20

                                                            96–42062
                                                                CIP
                                                                 AC

Printed in the United States of America
96 97 98 99 00 QBP 9 8 7 6 5 4 3 2 1

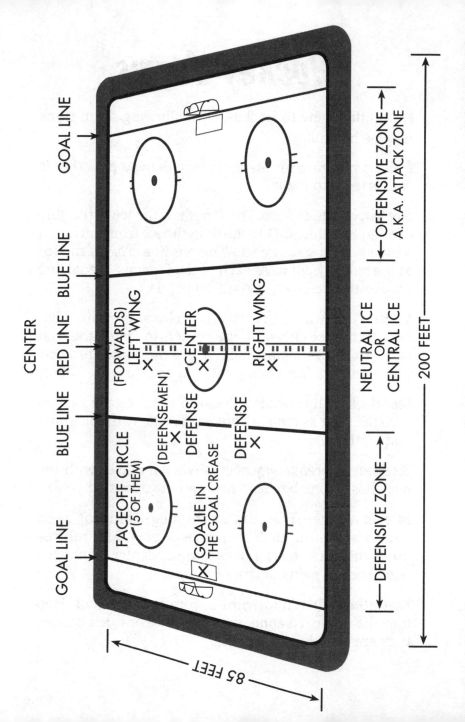

Hockey Terms

For readers new to hockey, the following definitions may be helpful.

Assist: A player earns an assist by making a pass that is converted into a goal.

Blue line, red line, goal line: The length of the ice is roughly divided into thirds. One third up the ice from each end a blue line crosses the ice. The red line crosses the ice at the halfway point. At each of the far ends, a goal line crosses the ice (see diagram on page v).

Boards: The entire ice surface is enclosed by waist-high boards that are curved in the corners to match the oval of the rink. A Plexiglas shield above the boards protects the spectators from being hit by a stray puck.

Body check: In hockey, it is legal to run into the person with the puck as long as contact is made with the upper body or hips.

Breakaway: A breakaway occurs when a player with the puck has no one between him and the opposing goalie.

Faceoff: A faceoff occurs at the beginning of each period and after each stoppage of play. The referee drops the puck to start play, and the center from each team tries to gain control of the puck.

Forechecker: When a forward or forwards are sent deep into the offensive zone after the puck or puck carrier, they are called forecheckers.

Hipcheck: A hipcheck is similar to a body check except contact is made as the hip is swung outward.

Icing: An icing penalty is called when a player shoots from behind his blue line and the puck travels all the way across the goal line at the far end. It results in a faceoff in the player's own end, which cancels the advantage of having moved the puck so far.

One-time: The process of hitting the puck without first stopping it.

Overtime: Overtime rules vary in different leagues. In the WHL, it consists of ten minutes of extra play. The first team to score in the extra time wins the game (called sudden-death overtime). In regular season play, a tie at the end of overtime remains a tie. In playoff games, overtime is played until a goal is scored to break the tie.

Period: A regular hockey game consists of sixty minutes of play, divided into three twenty-minute periods.

Point: (1) A single point is given for a goal. (2) In team standings, zero points are accumulated for a loss, one point for a tie, and two points for a win. (3) When a defenseman is standing inside the opposition's blue line, his position is also referred to as "standing at the point."

Power play: Penalties in hockey result in the offending player "serving time" in the penalty box. This time varies according to the penalty. With one and sometimes two fewer players on the ice, the penalized team is at a tremendous disadvantage. The unpenalized team is then considered on the power play. It is also known as a "man advantage" or a "two-man advantage."

Slap shot: A slap shot is the hardest shot in hockey. A player raises his stick above his shoulders before swinging downward to "slap" the shot. Slap shots have been recorded at speeds of well over 100 miles per hour.

Stickhandle: To control the puck by moving it from side to side with the blade of the hockey stick.

Two-on-one, three-on-one, four-on-one, and so on: If there is only one defenseman between the goalie and two attackers with the puck, it is called a "two-on-one"; the other numbers correspond to the various situations.

One

Because of a cowgirl named Stephanie Becker, I ended up wondering which would kill me first—a charging bull or a man with a rifle. But that was on a cold moonlit night in the mountains, long after we first met.

All of it really began ten months earlier at the end of the hockey season, when I saw her at an awards dinner for the Kamloops Blazers hockey team. I'll tell you right now, it wasn't the way I wanted to meet a beautiful girl.

It was one of those dinners with about five hundred people in one of those big hotel rooms used for wedding dances. The lights were low except for the spotlight on the stage. The man behind the microphone started, "This year's Most Valuable Player award goes to . . ."

The announcer wore a tuxedo that didn't hide his big belly. He spoke in the kind of low voice that people use when you know they love to hear themselves talk. He dragged out the suspense.

"Yes, folks, it's our final award of the evening. The one we've been waiting for. It goes to . . ."

He tried to add more suspense. Not that I felt any. Everyone knew the best player on our team was Luke Zannetti. He'd scored 212 points and led us to the Memorial Cup championship. Nobody liked him, but he didn't care. He didn't need to care. He had already been drafted by the Montreal Canadians, a team in the National Hockey League. That was one step up from our Tier One junior hockey team in the Western Hockey League. Of course, being drafted didn't guarantee he'd make the team. But the way Luke had been scoring, everyone was sure he'd be playing for the Canadians some day.

"Hey, Louie," someone shouted from the crowd. "Hurry up. Next season's almost here."

A bunch of people laughed.

Louie, whose face had the wrinkles of a bulldog, glared into the crowd. But the spotlight made it hard for him to see beyond the stage. As for me, I was watching a beautiful girl with long blond hair. She sat a few tables away, between me and the stage. I wondered who she was. Even though I didn't know her name, I knew that if she'd just look over and smile, I would ask her to marry me.

On the stage, Louie cleared his throat, hitched his pants, and finished. "The MVP award goes to the left winger, number 17 . . ."

Applause started as people heard the number. I frowned. That wasn't Luke's number. It was . . .

". . . yes, folks. Let's hear it for seventeen-year-old Josh Ellroy!"

I knew that name. I couldn't believe it. But I knew it. It was my name.

"Hey goofball." Gordie Penn, sitting beside me, elbowed my ribs. He elbows a lot of people but usually on the ice during hockey games. "Stand up. You're a star."

"Huh?" I'd won the MVP over Luke Zannetti?

He elbowed me again. "Come on, Cowboy. Stand up. People are staring."

I stood. People were not only staring at me, but they were also clapping. Somehow, with all those eyes staring at me, I had to get to the stage without tripping.

"Cowboy!" Gordie said. "Your coat!"

My sports coat was still on my chair. I'd taken it off because it was too hot. I didn't stop to put it on, though. I was too scared to think straight.

"'Atta boy, Cowboy," Dougie Metcalf called above the noise from another table. "You worked for it!"

Dougie was the center on my line. He'd helped me score 190 points. I tried to say something back to him, but my voice wouldn't even squeak. Nervousness and a dry throat do that to a person.

I stepped toward the stage. It seemed like I was moving in another person's body. A body with rubber legs. Up on the stage, I'd be standing in front of five hundred people. I'd have to speak in front of five hundred people.

The spotlight was on my face and chest as I walked

ahead. It was so bright that I could barely see a path. To pack everyone into the room, the round tables were squeezed close together with eight chairs around each. With the meals finished and people sitting back in their chairs, I had to turn sideways to get between the two tables ahead of me.

The clapping got louder. Sweat ran down my ribs from my armpits. This was a lot scarier than going into sudden-death overtime* in a crowded arena.

I took another rubbery step. I'd have to squeeze between two more pairs of tables. At one sat the beautiful girl and her long blond hair. Only in my dreams would I be able to say something cool to her as I walked by. I was so scared I'd barely be able to spit out my name.

More clapping. Some whistling. It hit me. Not only would I have to say something when I got the award, but there would also be a photographer from the newspaper. Did I look all right?

As I stumbled ahead, I smoothed my hair with my hands. I ran my tongue over my teeth checking for bits of food. I tightened my tie. There would be five hundred people watching me.

Five hundred.

I turned sideways and slipped between the next two tables.

"Hey, Ellroy," a man at one table said. "I voted for you."

---

* An asterisk in the text indicates a hockey term that is in the list of definitions on pages vi–viii.

In my fear, I hadn't noticed Pete Burrow, a sportswriter. In my fear, I didn't even think to say thanks. I kept walking.

One last thing to check. My zipper. I hooked my thumbs in my belt and pretended to hitch up my pants. I hoped no one would notice that I reached with a finger for the top of my zipper to make sure it was there.

I nearly fainted. All I felt was air. *My zipper was open, and I was about to face five hundred people.* I didn't even have a sports coat to cover me up.

But I couldn't do a thing. The spotlight was all over me. I wasn't going to stop in plain view of everyone and zip up.

I had an idea. The blond girl's table was next. As I turned sideways to get past her table, I could turn my back to the spotlight. That way no one would see me quickly yank my zipper into place.

I could rush the length of the ice in under a second, but this trip to the stage was taking forever. Finally, I reached the last set of tables—and the beautiful girl with long blond hair.

Her perfume reached my nose. So much for being a cool hero. Instead, I was an idiot with an open fly.

I turned sideways, facing the back of her chair. The spotlight was finally off my face. I tried to time it right. I zipped quickly as I kept moving sideways. I stumbled a bit as I turned to the spotlight again, almost tripping.

I took another step. I heard a yelp behind me, but I couldn't stop to see what had happened. Not with everyone staring at me. Maybe I'd stepped on someone's foot and in my nervousness didn't feel it. I hoped it wasn't the girl's foot.

Finally I reached the steps to the stage. The guy in the tuxedo grinned at me. A weird grin. Did he think I would trip as I walked up the steps? Somehow I made it up the steps. I moved across the stage and shook hands with Mr. Tuxedo. Then I faced the crowd. Just me, a microphone, and the MVP trophy in my right hand.

All I saw were the outlines and shadows of lots of people.

"This is a, um, big surprise," I said. I stopped. I didn't know what else to say.

"I'll say it's a surprise," someone yelled. Probably the same guy who had yelled at the announcer earlier. "Look down!"

Laughter started from somewhere, like a little wave from the back. It grew louder.

I told myself I had zipped my fly. I took a quick peek down anyway. And nearly died.

All I could see was blond hair. The blond hair of a wig. Caught in my zipper in front of five hundred people.

Blond hair.

I looked over at the girl's table. She wasn't there. In the shadows at the back, I saw someone run out of the room holding a program over her head.

She had been wearing a wig? The wig that was now stuck in my zipper?

I tried to smile at the five hundred people. I couldn't imagine how this could get worse.

I yanked at the wig. It didn't budge. I yanked harder. I heard a rip that echoed across the room through the microphone.

It had just gotten worse. Not only was the wig still stuck, but now I had also ripped the seam of my pants.

Finally, someone had the sense to shut the spotlight off. I walked off the stage with laughter roaring all around me.

And that was only the beginning of my problems with Stephanie.

Two

For the next ten months, every time I looked at my MVP award I wanted to call her to say I was sorry. But I didn't know her name. We had never met. We didn't go to the same high school. And she probably hated me. I figured it would be crazy to call.

Besides, what would I say? *Sorry I pulled your wig off in front of five hundred people? Sorry I let it hang from my zipper? And by the way, why were you wearing a stupid wig in the first place?*

So, day after day, whenever I thought of the awards dinner, I tried to think of hockey instead.

That should have been easy.

At the end of the last season, I'd been a draft pick for the Buffalo Sabres, a National Hockey League team. By drafting me, they had secured the rights to me as a player. But it didn't mean I'd automatically make the team.

To improve my chances to play pro hockey, I wanted

to be heavier and stronger. So each summer day after working on my dad's cattle ranch, I pumped weights and dreamed about playing for the Sabres.

Training camp for the Kamloops Blazers started late in August. I moved back into town from the ranch to play hockey. After that came the regular season. We practiced or played hockey almost every day through the fall and winter. Toward the end of the season, the team was in a tight race for first place. I was also in a tight race for leading scorer in the league. Luke Zannetti, who was playing bad and had hardly scored in two months, wasn't even in the race. What else was there to think about?

Some girl with blond hair who probably hated me, that's what.

I mean, I tried to fool myself. I told myself that I didn't care. But it bugged me that I never had a chance to say I was sorry. I found myself looking for her in most places I went in Kamloops. If I saw someone with blond hair on the street or in a shopping mall, I'd hope it was her.

But in ten months, I never did find her.

She found me.

Three

It was during a hockey practice on an afternoon in February. Half the team played against the other half. Red jerseys against blue. There were ten minutes left in the game. I wore a red jersey. Skating along the boards*, I tried to get the puck from my friend Gordie Penn, who wore blue.

He elbowed my head.

"Hey," I said, pushing him against the boards. I mushed his head into the Plexiglas. "This is practice!"

"Just trying to look good," he said. He grunted and pushed me off him. "There's a babe watching us. Take a look."

"Not now," I said, pushing him back into the boards. "I'm busy."

"Busy?" he panted.

"Yup. Busy making you look bad." I kicked the puck away from him and chased it.

Gordie grabbed my sweater and hung on as I dragged

him. It didn't bother me. I'd added a lot of bulk by working out with weights all summer.

Ten steps ahead, Luke Zannetti was almost open for a pass. There was only one defenseman between us. Gordie was laughing as he hung on to my sweater. But I knew if I took one more big step, I'd be able to flick the puck into the air and put it just in front of Luke.

Which I did.

It was a perfect pass. It should have sent him in all alone for an easy goal. Except when the puck hit Luke's stick, he tripped. The puck kept going and Luke slid on his stomach. It was the kind of sloppy hockey he'd been playing for the last couple of months.

Everyone on the ice laughed at him.

Coach Price blew the whistle and told us to take a breather.

It took Luke a few minutes to get up.

I skated over to him, taking off my helmet to get some fresh air.

"Next time," I said, "I'll slow my pass down. Hate to knock you over like that."

I was joking. I thought Zannetti could tell I was joking. We weren't friends or anything. Luke didn't have any friends. Still, because I was smiling, I thought he could see I was just kidding.

Instead of laughing, he dropped his gloves and swung at me.

His fist hit me solid on the side of my face. I fell to my knees. He jumped on my back and started pounding my head. It had happened so fast I didn't have a chance.

It seemed like he pounded me for a long time before someone dragged him off of me.

I slowly got back to my feet. A couple of guys were holding him back. A couple of guys held me too. I wasn't going to fight, though. Hockey is a team game.

"What is going through your head?" I shouted. I could taste blood. I could also feel a marble-sized lump on my bottom lip. "If you can't play hockey, don't take it out on me!"

"Shut your mouth, Cowboy!" he shouted back. Luke's eyes were wild. He was a little taller than me but not quite as heavy. A lot of girls liked him because he was good looking with dark, wavy hair. Not many guys liked him because all he cared about was himself.

Coach Price skated between me and Zannetti. Coach Price had a buzz haircut and a bent nose. He was wide too. He had spent five years in the NHL as a defenseman before becoming our coach.

"Knock it off," he barked.

"Coach, he—" I tried to say.

"Knock it off," Coach told me. "I don't want to hear a word."

He turned to Zannetti. "And you know better. You're the team captain."

"But—" Zannetti tried to say.

"But nothing," Coach Price said. "We'll talk later."

Coach spun on his skates and blew his whistle. "Five minutes of hard skating," he said. "Fun time is over."

Everyone groaned. He rolled his eyes and shook his head. That's one of the good things about Coach Price.

He doesn't expect us to be silent robots. As long as we do what he tells us, we can kid around and he'll kid back.

So we all started skating laps. Fast then slow, depending on how many times he blasted his whistle. As we skated off the ice at the end of practice, I finally saw the girl Gordie had been talking about.

It was the blond girl from the awards dinner. She was standing near the exit off the ice. We all had to pass her to get to the dressing room. Her light hair was a lot shorter than the blond wig, but it was the same girl. I could hardly believe it.

I thought of my bleeding lip and how she had seen me get beat up. I felt like a fool.

One by one, the guys on the team passed her. She ignored them.

My turn came. I tried to look the other way as I stepped off the ice. Maybe she wouldn't notice me.

It didn't work.

"Are you Josh?" she asked.

A couple of the guys behind me hooted.

She frowned at them and they shut up.

Great. The first time we had met, I'd pulled her wig off. The second time, she'd watched me get beat up.

"Yes," I said. "I'm Josh. The guys call me Cowboy."

I rubbed my nose like it itched and kept my hand in front of my mouth. It was the only thing I could think of to hide my bleeding lip.

"Stephanie Becker." She held out a piece of paper. "My phone number. Can we get together this weekend?"

I took it. There was more hooting from the guys behind me waiting to get off the ice. This time I turned around and shut them up with a dirty look.

"That'd be great. But the team's going on a road trip for some out-of-town games," I said. "We don't get back until late Saturday. And I promised my parents I would drive out to the ranch to visit all day Sunday."

"Monday then?" she asked. "Please? Call me on Sunday night if you can. We really need to talk."

"About what?" I asked.

"It's so crazy I can't tell you unless we have lots of time."

"After practice today? I can meet you at McDonald's."

She shook her head no. Her eyes were a pale, pale blue. They looked pretty with her blond hair. Very pretty.

"I can't right now," she said. "I'm supposed to get back to my folks' ranch."

She lived on a ranch too? I liked her even more.

"Promise you'll call me Sunday night," she said. "I want to talk as soon as possible."

Like I was going to say no?

"Sure," I said. "Sunday night. We'll get together on Monday."

But, as it turned out, Monday was too late.

 *Four*

Tell you what, Joshua," Dad said, "you won't find any place in the world prettier than this."

"Yup," I said, blowing on my hands to keep them warm.

It was Sunday afternoon. Sunday mornings on the ranch were for church and family, and I had enjoyed the peace and quiet after the road trip. Now Dad and I were on horseback in the bright sun. We had ridden to the top of a hill and were looking down on the valley. Dad was right. It was pretty.

Our ranch was about a half hour drive southeast of the city of Kamloops, the biggest city in the interior mountains of British Columbia. The ranch covered most of the bottomlands of the valley. It also stretched high into the hills where we were sitting on our horses. There were bigger ranches around, but not many. We had 3,000 head of cattle on over 50,000 acres. Our work crew ranged from twenty to forty cowboys, depending on the time of year.

It had been a light year for snow, and most of the ground was exposed. As far as we could see, pine trees dotted the hills like dark green crayons standing tall on rolling brown paper. Behind the hills the peaks of the mountains cut against the blue bowl of the sky. They weren't as big and impressive as some of the Rocky Mountains farther east, but they were still pretty.

"Son," Dad said as we admired the view, "I'd like to pass all this on to you someday. I sure hope you make this ranch your home when you finish with hockey."

My horse stamped the ground. It wanted to keep moving. The air was cool, and I could see the horse's breath as it snorted.

Dad grinned. "But I hope you play hockey for a long time before you get back here."

"Me too," I said. "I think if I can keep near the top of the scoring race, I'll have a real good chance at making the Sabres next fall."

"It seems like it's going well," he said. "But your mother fussed over you so much this morning, we really haven't had a chance to talk."

"It's been a pretty good season," I told him. "You probably heard the out-of-town games on the radio."

"Three games, three wins," he said. "And four goals and six assists* for you. Sure I've been listening."

Dad moved his horse forward. I stayed beside him as we followed a wide path down the hill. I was as big as Dad now. In the saddle, all I had to do was look over to see his face at my level.

Under his cowboy hat, he has gray in his black hair.

He also has deep wrinkles around his eyes. Except for the gray and the wrinkles, we look close to the same. He has a bigger nose than I do—almost too big—but his face is wide, so it seems the right size. Mom teases us about our big dimples when we smile.

"What's going on with Luke Zannetti?" he asked. "It sounds like the guy can't do anything right."

Without thinking, I licked my lip. It was still sore where he had punched me earlier in the week.

"Luke's played better," I said. "But his head is so big, he won't talk to anyone. But then, he never has. You know that."

"Remember that, son," Dad said. "You can be the best hockey player in the world, but it's who you are that counts."

"Yes sir," I said.

"They made him team captain because he's older. They made you assistant captain because they respect you," he said. "They also voted you MVP last year because they respect you more than him. Don't lose that respect."

I tilted my cowboy hat back and scratched my head. "Dad?"

Our horses picked their way down the hill. I swayed in the saddle with the movement.

"Yes?"

"Each of the last four times I've visited the ranch, you've said that same thing."

He laughed. "And I'll keep saying it. It's part of my job as your father."

He pointed toward the top of another hill. "Let's go that way. I want to check on Big Boy. I wanted him to get some exercise, so we've got him fenced in with a small herd."

Big Boy was our world-class Limousin bull. Ranchers from all over paid five thousand dollars each time they used him for breeding. Generally we kept him in a barn near the ranch house. He had cost $150,000 at an auction, and it wouldn't be smart to let him roam the hills.

"Exercise?" I asked.

"He's seemed a bit slow lately," Dad said. Another grin. "Nothing like fresh air in the mountains to make you feel better. Right?"

"Right." When I was in the hills away from hockey, I missed hockey. When I was playing hockey and away from the hills, I missed the ranch. I missed seeing Big Boy too. I remember when he was hardly more than a calf, and I was a lot smaller myself. I used to ride him and then feed him.

I think Big Boy remembered those days too, because he never did anything mean toward me. Not that I'd try to ride him again. He weighed over a thousand pounds. Think of a small truck. That was Big Boy.

Before I could say anything about Big Boy, Dad pointed ahead of us.

"See it, son? A coyote."

I did see it. It was down the hill near a stand of trees. About the size of a German shepherd dog, it had a big, bushy tail. It stared back at us as we rode closer.

"That's one smart animal," Dad said. "It knows I don't have a rifle. Otherwise it would be long gone."

"I wonder what it's eating," I said. "Looks like it's standing beside some kind of dead animal."

Dad frowned. "I hope it isn't what I think it is."

We rode closer. The coyote slipped into the bushes. Where it had been standing lay a dead cow. Blood was smeared on the grass around it.

"It is what I thought it was," Dad said. "This isn't good. Coyotes aren't big enough to bring down cattle."

My horse tried to turn away. It must have smelled the blood.

"Dad," I said. "Over there."

I pointed at more dead cows, half hidden in the dips of the land.

Dad let out a deep breath. "Six," he said after a long pause. "Six dead. This isn't the time of year for bear. I can't believe wolves are back in the valley. What is going on?"

He lowered himself from his horse and tied the reins to a tree branch. I did the same with my horse. We walked toward the first dead animal.

We didn't like what we saw. Someone had taken an ax and chopped at it. Blood and bones and guts and cowhide were scattered everywhere.

"This is sick!" I half shouted. "Who would do this? And why?"

"Six thousand dollars," Dad said quietly. "Each animal is worth a thousand dollars. Six dead. Six thousand dollars. That's what someone has cost us."

Dad was wrong. It cost far more. Over the next hill, we found twelve more dead. That was another twelve thousand dollars.

Then, on the other side of the fence, we found Big Boy. Someone had chopped him up just as bad as the others. A hundred and fifty thousand dollars' worth of prize bull was now twenty dollars' worth of dog food.

Five

Weird and terrible as it was to find the dead cattle, I still had to play hockey. Monday afternoon, I was back at the Riverside Coliseum for practice.

I didn't say much as I put on my hockey equipment in the dressing room. It really bothered me what someone had done to Big Boy and the other cattle.

Who? Why?

It worried me so much that I barely remembered getting dressed. I was leaning forward to tie my skates when Dougie Metcalf came over and sat beside me.

"Watch the telephone," he whispered.

I didn't get it. Why was he whispering?

I looked around the dressing room. Guys looked back at me and grinned. That told me something was happening, but I couldn't guess what.

I watched the telephone. We had a big dressing room. Each of us had a place to hang our equipment between games and practices. At one end was the shower area.

At the other a telephone hung on the wall. It was used mainly by Coach Price or the trainer or assistant coaches.

The telephone rang.

Gordie Penn jumped up. He already had his skates on, and he clunked toward the telephone. He answered it before Coach Price could reach it.

Gordie listened. He shook his head to let Coach Price know it wasn't for him. Coach went out to the rink to get ready for practice.

"Hey, Luke," Gordie said. "It's for you."

"Yeah, yeah," Luke said from his corner of the dressing room. "If it's the Montreal Canadians, tell them I can start tomorrow."

"Fat chance," Dougie whispered. "Luke's hurting our team more than he's helping. I wonder why Coach Price lets him keep playing."

Luke walked over to the telephone and took it from Gordie.

"Hello?" Luke said. He frowned. "Hello?"

Dougie kept whispering to me. "Johnny Smith is calling from a pay phone down the hall. He's speaking soft, so Luke can barely hear him."

"Why?" I whispered back. Johnny Smith was one of our defensemen. I noticed a lot of guys in the dressing room were trying to hide smiles as they watched Luke on the telephone.

"Hello?" Luke said again. He pressed the phone against his head. He was getting mad. "Hello?"

"Why is Johnny speaking softly on the other end?"

Dougie said back to me. "So Luke will press the phone against his ear."

"Well," I said, "that explains it."

Dougie could tell I didn't mean it, and he grinned at me. "Are you kidding? Before you got here, Gordie put heat rub on the phone."

"Huh?"

"Heat rub. You know, the stuff that—"

"I know what it is," I said. It was a thick lotion that you put on your skin over sore muscles. It smelled like spearmint and warmed up until it was hot. Sweat and water only made it feel hotter. If you could help it, you never put it on before a game. You used it after, when you needed the heat to help your muscles. "But why would he . . ."

I stopped myself from asking the rest of my question. I suddenly knew why.

"Hello? Hello? Speak up!" He pressed the phone against his head so hard it looked like he was trying to screw it on. "I can't hear you!"

Now Luke was really mad. He slammed the phone down and marched back to his corner of the dressing room. He looked at all of us as he sat down. "You'd think a person would be able to raise his voice."

"You'd think," Gordie Penn agreed.

The rest of the guys tried to look innocent. They all knew what I knew about the heat rub. They all knew what Luke didn't know. At least what Luke didn't know yet.

This wasn't a good sign for Luke. A year ago, no one would have dared to play a trick like this on him. Tricks were something you played on rookies to make them part of the team. Tricks were not something you played on the older guys. Not unless you were trying to tell the older guys they *weren't* part of the team.

I shot a quick look over at Luke. Everyone else was waiting too.

It started with his shoulder. Luke jerked his shoulder up to rub it against his ear. A few seconds later, he frowned and rubbed his ear with his hand.

A few of the guys giggled.

Luke rubbed harder. His face was scrunched up.

"Hey!" Luke rubbed really, really hard. "This is hot!"

It busted up the team. Most of the guys started to howl with laughter.

Luke stood up and danced around, pressing his hand against his ear. The heat rub from the telephone must have been all over the tender skin of his ear. I couldn't imagine how hot it felt.

Everyone laughed as Luke ran toward the shower area for cold water. We knew it wouldn't help. Nothing got heat rub off once it was on.

"How'd you like that one?" Dougie asked me. "It was Gordie's idea."

"Great," I said. But I wasn't laughing much. Big Boy was dead, along with eighteen other cattle. Not even a telephone trick made me feel any better.

Telephone!

I'd forgotten to call Stephanie Becker.

I wondered if she would understand.

I called her as soon as practice ended. She understood all too well how all those dead, chopped up animals would make me forget to call earlier. The same thing had happened on her ranch the month before.

Six

"Let me get this straight," I said to Stephanie. "Somebody did the same thing on your ranch? Killed cattle?"

"Just like I told you on the phone this afternoon," Stephanie said. "About a month ago. And that's what I wanted to talk to you about. Only now it seems too late."

It was Monday night. We were in the McDonald's restaurant along the TransCanada highway. Traffic outside was busy, with big trucks gearing down and gearing up on their way in and out of Kamloops.

I had been a big spender, buying us four chocolate milkshakes. When she said she only wanted one, I had told her I'd better drink the other three so they didn't get wasted. That had made her smile.

I drank the first milkshake. I have this habit of staring in the distance when I think. I was thinking about our dead cattle and the dead cattle on her ranch.

I stared at the wall behind her and thought about how weird it was.

She caught me staring. She thought I was staring at her, not past her. "I know," she said, "you're wondering about my hair. Before we talk about the ranch, maybe there's something else we should talk about? Like an awards dinner last year?"

I felt my face turn red.

"Good milkshake, isn't it," I said, finishing off the first one. "Maybe I'll have another."

I grabbed the second one.

"Don't try to change the subject. Ever since the dinner, I've wanted to call you to say I was sorry."

"You? Call me? Sorry?"

"I think it was worse for you than me," she said. "Nobody noticed me with my program over my head. You . . ." she began to laugh. "You were on stage with a wig stuck in your fly."

"Very funny," I said. "The guys still tell me to check my zipper. Why were you wearing a wig, anyway?"

"A bad hair day. A real bad hair day."

"Pardon me?"

"It's a girl thing. You see, my dad is a huge Blazers fan. He planned to take me and my mom to the dinner. I thought I would do something special and get my hair permed for it."

Stephanie touched her hair. "Look how short it is now."

"Yes?"

"The day before the dinner I went to a beauty salon.

It was the worst thing that could have happened. To perm hair, they put it in curlers and soak it in chemicals."

"You're right," I said. "It's a girl thing. Guys would never do that."

"But they'll stand in front of a television and yell at athletes and refs who can't hear them."

"Your perm?" I said. "We don't need to talk about guys."

"They had a new girl working at the salon. She mixed the wrong chemicals together. It became like an acid and burned off most of my hair."

"Seriously?" I began to laugh.

"Not funny," she said. "I was sitting under the hair dryer, and all of a sudden there was smoke everywhere. My hair was ruined, so I had to wear a wig until it grew long enough for a shorter style. That took a month. Even now, almost a year later, it's not nearly as long as it used to be."

"Thank you," I said. "I've been going nuts wondering why you had a wig on."

"Why didn't you call and ask?"

I finished my second milkshake and reached for the third. "Afraid you might shoot me. Plus, I didn't know your name."

"I'll forgive you if you forgive me." She reached across the table to shake my hand.

"It's a deal," I said. I liked how warm her hand was. We held on long enough for both of us to know we had held on a little too long. I felt my face growing red again.

"So," I said, coughing as I let go. "Um, you live on a ranch."

She explained that she lived about thirty miles northwest of Kamloops. Since our ranch was as far southeast of Kamloops, she lived nearly sixty miles away from me. That explained why I had not run into her during the last ten months.

She described how they had found their dead cattle. Fifteen had been killed, including their Limousin bull, Champion. All the cattle, and Champion, had been chopped up. She'd hated all the blood.

"The police think it might be people in a cult," she said.

"Cult," I echoed.

"You know, witches. People making sacrifices at night."

I shivered. It wasn't just the cold milkshake. "Creepy."

"It's real strange," she said. "Is it easy to get to the area where Big Boy was killed?"

"Nope," I said. "And that's something Dad and I can't figure out. There's no way to drive there. We're wondering how the killers got in and out. It would be hard to ride horses at night. And we didn't find any tracks."

"Same with our ranch," Stephanie said. "I can't see any city folks going to all that trouble."

"If they were witches," I said, grinning, "they could have flown in on broomsticks."

She didn't grin back. "That would be the only way. We'd hear an airplane or helicopter if it flew into the valley."

Since my little joke didn't work, I gave my attention to my third and last milkshake.

"Anyway," Stephanie said, "I wanted to talk to you last week about this. It was so strange that I didn't want to just tell you over the telephone."

I sucked so hard on my straw that it made a noise when I reached the bottom of the milkshake. Hoping Stephanie hadn't noticed, I said, "That's what I don't get. You wanted to talk to me last week—*before* Big Boy and the other cattle died. How could you even guess?"

She looked around the restaurant and dropped her voice. "Bloodlines."

"Bloodlines." I repeated it. I knew what she was talking about. Big Boy was a registered bull. We could trace his bloodline not only to his parents, but also to all four of his grandparents, all eight of his great-grandparents, and all sixteen of his great-great grandparents. That was part of why Big Boy had been so expensive.

"Bloodlines. I'm guessing you know Big Boy was sired by a bull named Locomotive."

I wondered how she knew Locomotive was Big Boy's father. "I might play hockey," I said, "but there's a reason my friends call me Cowboy. Ranching is important to me."

"You might not know this," she said. "Our bull, Champion, was also sired by Locomotive. Big Boy and Champion were half brothers. They were both worth hundreds of thousands of dollars."

"That is strange," I said. "Still, just because Champion

was killed, why did you think it would happen to Big Boy? Why did you think you needed to warn me?"

"Why?" Stephanie's voice dropped even more. She leaned forward. "Because last week I found out this has also happened to two other bulls sired by Locomotive."

"What!"

She nodded. "Yes. On a ranch in Alberta, and on another ranch in Montana. It's like someone is going around North America trying to kill the entire bloodline."

Seven

As I fell asleep that night, I thought about what I had learned by the end of my evening with Stephanie Becker.

A week earlier, Stephanie had read in a cattle magazine that ranchers in southern Alberta were worried about their animals. There had been some strange killings. The cattle there had been chopped up the same way as Big Boy and Champion. When she'd read about a prize bull being killed, she had noticed Locomotive's name as the father.

That had made her start asking around. She'd called the Canadian Limousin Association to get the names and owners of other bulls in the bloodline. That's when she found out about the killings in Montana.

The rancher in Montana was half convinced it had been done by UFOs. One of his workers had reported seeing a strange glow in the sky and hearing a distant roar.

Stephanie had told her father everything.

He had agreed that it was strange. He had also said that she read too many mystery books in her spare time. He'd pointed out that their bull was dead. The insurance money had covered it. She shouldn't make a fool of herself looking into the business of other people.

But Stephanie was too angry that Champion had been killed. She wasn't going to quit. On her list of owners of other bulls in the bloodline, she'd seen the Ellroy ranch. She had decided to warn me about the other killings on the crazy chance someone might try to do the same to Big Boy.

Only now, it wasn't such a crazy chance.

Only now, she wanted to find out more, so she could get the police involved.

Only now, she wanted me to help.

# Eight

The next night, we were scheduled for a home game against the Medicine Hat Tigers. It was a usual day for me. I got up at around 7:00. I had breakfast with my billets, the Dickersons, who were paid by the Kamloops Blazers to give me room and board. I went to school. All through the day, I kept thinking about Stephanie Becker and what she'd told me about someone trying to kill Locomotive's bloodline.

I should have been thinking about hockey.

The Blazers were favored to win, but it wouldn't be easy. The Medicine Hat Tigers are always a tough team. Most of their guys are big and love to skate hard and hit hard. We had to skate and play just as hard. I was also hoping to get a couple more goals or assists to keep me near the top of the scoring race.

I got to the arena early and was the first person in the dressing room. I wanted to get mentally ready to play. I thought it would help if I put myself in a place where I had no choice but to think of hockey.

It might have worked, except Luke Zannetti was the second person in the dressing room. And he had shaved his head—totally bald.

No kidding. Totally bald.

All he needed was a big number on the back of his head. It would have looked like a giant pool ball resting on his shoulders. He was so bald that his skull was shiny.

My hockey thoughts stopped being hockey thoughts.

"What are you staring at?" he snarled as he hung his coat up.

"Well," I said, making sure I smiled so he'd see I was joking. I wasn't scared of him. I just wanted to make sure our team played as a team. "If I were standing right beside you, I guess I'd be staring at a reflection of myself off your head. That's some haircut."

"Michael Jordon shaves his head," Luke told me. "It's something that only the coolest athletes do."

I didn't have a chance to answer because Coach Price walked into the dressing room.

"Hey, guys," he said. If he noticed that Luke was bald, he didn't say anything about it. "Glad you're both here. I need to talk to the two of you."

"About what?" Luke said. "You and I already talked about the fight in practice."

Coach Price frowned at his rudeness. "We're going to mix up the lines tonight."

I nodded, wondering why he was telling us. Maybe because Luke was the captain and I was one of the team's two assistant captains.

"Cowboy," Coach said to me. "Luke is moving down from the first line to play center on your line. We're going to move Dougie up to play center on the first line."

On our team, the first two lines were equally strong. It didn't mean Luke was moving "down." But it did mean he and I would be playing together.

And I didn't want him on my line. This was the guy who had flipped out in practice over a small joke. The guy who had punched me in the mouth. Worse, even when he was at his best, he wasn't much of a team player. All he wanted was to score his own goals. That meant he sometimes hung on to the puck instead of making a smart pass. And Luke wasn't at his best. Everyone knew that.

I didn't say any of this to Coach Price. Dad had taught me to accept new situations and make the best of them without complaining.

"What?" Luke said. "I haven't played second line for years."

"Starting tonight you will," Coach Price told him. "Cowboy is one of the strongest left wingers in the league. He's a great anchor for the second line, and I think this shift will be good for the team. And for both of you."

Coach Price stopped and cleared his throat. "There's a slight problem, though. With this change, no one on first line will have an A or a C."

I knew instantly where Coach Price was going. If there is a disputed call, only the captain or one of the two assistant captains can talk to the ref. The coach can't. Often, the player will get instructions from the coach on what to ask the ref. Coach Price needed a captain or an assistant on the ice at all times. With Luke and me now on the same line . . .

"Cowboy?" he asked. "Mind letting Dougie wear the A for a while?"

"Sure, Coach." I'd worked hard to get the A for assistant captain on my jersey. But I tried to agree cheerfully. Coach Price was going to do it anyway. There was no sense complaining about something I couldn't change.

Coach nodded, then left us alone. I didn't have much to say to Luke. But it didn't matter. Other players started to arrive. They teased Luke about his new shaved look. That left me alone to worry about Big Boy, Stephanie Becker, whether we would win the game, and what it would be like to play on a line with Luke.

Nine

Coach Price was wrong about the line change being good for me and Luke. From the beginning of the game, I skated until I thought my legs would drop off. It didn't seem to make any difference. Whenever I got the puck, Luke was out of position to take a pass.

That basically meant I had no one to pass to. At left wing, I was usually too far away to make a pass to Gordie Penn, my right winger. His position was on the other side of the ice. Passing cross ice is hardly ever smart. Too many other players can step in and take the puck.

Luke, at center, was skating as if someone had strapped a bag of potatoes to his back. I would go into the boards with one of the Medicine Hat Tigers and fight for the puck. I'd come out, lift my head to look for Luke, and see him two steps behind their center. Not two steps ahead where I could pass.

Time and again, while I delayed and waited to make

a play, one or two of the Tigers would jump all over me. It was driving me crazy.

With five minutes left in the third period*, the score was tied at three. The right defense for the Tigers—the guy on my side of the ice—had the puck in the center ice area.

Luke made a move toward him, and the defenseman peeled away, still with the puck. He didn't see me coming in from the other side. I was able to ram him with my shoulder. He fell down. I didn't.

The puck was there, at my feet.

I heard Luke yell. He was skating toward the net. The other Tigers' defenseman was caught up the ice. There was no one between Luke and the goalie.

The Tigers' defenseman was getting to his knees and reaching for the puck with his stick. I stepped over his stick, pulled the puck toward me. I flipped it ahead of Luke, so he could reach it without slowing down.

The puck slapped the tape of his stick. It was a perfect pass. Luke was all alone on the goalie. The nearest Tigers' player was the left defenseman, who was at least five steps behind.

The crowd roared as fans jumped to their feet. *Three to three and we had a breakaway*!

Two strides later, Luke reached their blue line*.

I was following, but not part of, the play. This was Luke's chance to score and put us ahead. I'd be happy getting a point* for the assist.

But a stride later, the Tigers' defenseman was suddenly only three steps back of Luke.

I couldn't believe it. Luke was supposed to be one of the fastest players in the league. The Montreal Canadians wanted him, he was so fast. And a big defenseman was catching up to him?

Two steps later, the defenseman was breathing down Luke's back.

Two more steps and the defenseman was able to reach his stick around and knock the puck off Luke's stick.

The crowd's roar changed to groans. Luke hadn't even gotten close enough to fire a shot at the goalie.

Gordie, over on the right wing, slammed his stick against the ice in disappointment.

Luke?

Luke was so angry he spun around and punched the Tigers' defenseman. The referee put his hand up for a penalty against us. A few seconds later, he blew the whistle to stop the play.

Not only had Luke missed the breakaway, but he also took a penalty.

It hurt us bad. While we were one man short, the Tigers scored to make it 4–3 for them.

That's how the game ended.

In the dressing room, I didn't say a word. I didn't have to. The total silence of all the players was loud enough for Luke to know what we thought.

Ten

Stephanie was waiting for me as some of us walked out of the arena together after an early afternoon practice the next day. She was in the parking lot, standing beside an old, black Bronco 4 x 4.

"Ho, ho," Gordie said, elbowing me as usual. "Check out Miss America. I think she's looking for a certain Cowboy."

"Ho, ho," I said, "how will you look with a squashed nose?"

Gordie, two inches taller than me and a lot heavier, nicely decided to let me get away with that remark. Instead, he said, "I'd still look a lot better than Luke the Cuke."

The guys had started calling him Cuke, rhyming it with *Luke*. It was short for Cucumber. His head looked like the end of a giant cucumber. Luke, of course, ignored everyone. That was Luke's style. When he'd been one of the best players in the league, he got away with being

41

a jerk. Now that he was slipping, the guys didn't think he was cool.

I waved at Stephanie and stepped away from my teammates.

"Hi," I said.

"Hi," she said.

For some reason, both of us got a little shy.

After a long silence, I looked up at the clear sky. "Nice day," I said.

She laughed. "Is it a nice day to go for a drive?"

"Sure."

"Don't you want to know where?" she asked.

"Sure." I wasn't going to tell her that it would have been all right if we just drove circles around the parking lot.

"To your ranch," she said. "If we're lucky, there will still be a couple hours of daylight when we get there."

"Sure," I said.

"Don't you want to know why?" she asked.

"Sure."

Some of the guys were shouting at us as they got into their cars, the way guys do when they want to give you a rough time. I ignored them. So did she.

"I'd like to look over the spot where Big Boy and the other cattle were killed," she said.

"What are we looking for? My dad called in the police, and they already went over everything."

Dad had already filed an insurance claim. Part of the claim needed a police report. With it, he was going to get nearly all of the money that Big Boy had been worth.

"Did the police find anything?"

"Pieces of cattle," I answered. "Some footprints. Nothing else to give them any idea of who or why."

"Let's look around anyway," she said. "Maybe over a bigger area. The police didn't know about the other bloodline killings. They might not have searched real hard."

"Shouldn't we tell them about the other killings?" I asked.

"I already have," she told me. The sun on her face made a pretty picture. "This afternoon, before I stopped by here. They didn't sound too excited. I think partly because it sounds weird and partly because they aren't going to take a teenage girl very seriously."

"I will," I said.

"You will what?"

"Take you seriously." I realized what I was saying. "I mean . . . I'll take what you say seriously. I didn't mean get serious with you."

She frowned as she tried to decide what I was getting at.

"It's not that I think you're ugly," I said quickly. I wished I'd kept my mouth shut. "You're not. Oh boy, you're not. But you probably have lots of guys chasing you. I didn't mean I want to get serious with you. Because I don't want you to think I'd do something stupid like try to ask you out when you probably have a boyfriend. I mean—"

"Cowboy," she said, stopping me.

"Yes?" My ears were burning.

"You're cute."

My ears got hotter.

"Get in," she said, motioning toward her Bronco. "I'll drive. You give me directions on how to get to the ranch."

After we had both buckled our seatbelts, she started the engine. She put the Bronco in drive, but kept her foot on the brake. She turned toward me.

"And Josh?"

"Yes?"

She smiled. "I don't have a boyfriend."

Eleven

When Stephanie and I got to the ranch, we didn't stop by the house to visit because Mom and Dad were in town getting their weekly supplies.

So we drove right to the barn. I got out of the Bronco first and walked into the barn ahead of Stephanie. It was nice to smell horses and hay again.

One of our hired men was inside, shoveling horse manure into a wheelbarrow.

"Hello, Ernest," I said. "Just here to go for a ride with a friend."

He looked up at me and grunted. Ernest was a middle-aged guy with a skinny face wrinkled from a lot of wind and sun. Ernest used to be in the rodeo. He walked with a limp. A horse had once kicked his knee and broken the kneecap. I didn't know Ernest's last name because he had only started working at the ranch a few weeks earlier.

Stephanie walked into the barn behind me. "Josh, I hope you get me a fast horse."

Ernest dropped his shovel at the sight of her. I didn't blame him. Stephanie can do that to a person. Ernest grunted again as he picked up the shovel. He set it against the wall, put his head down, and pushed the wheelbarrow out of the barn.

"A fast horse?" I said to Stephanie. "You got it."

Stephanie wasn't listening. "Weird," she mumbled, more to herself than to me. She was watching Ernest push the wheelbarrow outside. "I think I've seen that guy before."

"Ernest?"

"Maybe not," she said. "I'd remember a name like that. Still, the way he walks . . ."

She smiled. "Where's my fast horse?"

I showed Stephanie a brown eight-year-old gelding. I pointed out where to find the saddle and reins. Then I saddled my own horse, Blazer. I was twelve years old when I got him, and there was never any question about what his name would be. Even then I dreamed of playing hockey for the Kamloops Blazers.

It only took about twenty minutes to get the horses saddled. We had about two hours of sunlight left when we began to ride toward the hill country where Big Boy had been killed.

As soon as we got to open grass, I moved my horse into a trot.

Stephanie was a good rider. Actually, she was a great

rider. The fast way to find out if someone knows how to ride is to watch them when the horse trots. A trot is very, very bouncy. Bad riders pound up and down in the saddle. Good riders stay glued to the saddle and move at the waist.

After a few minutes of trotting, she leaned forward and started to gallop her horse. I didn't have any choice but to keep up.

My horse Blazer is not only cow-smart but also big and tough and fast. I began to pass Stephanie.

"Hey!" she shouted, laughing. "No fair!"

I love the feel of riding a horse at full gallop. The wind rushes into your ears. You rise and fall with the drumming of horse hooves. It's almost as much fun as moving up the ice with the puck on your stick and the crowd screaming at your back.

A few minutes later, though, I pulled up on the reins for a couple of reasons. The first was safety. Horses gallop at more than twenty miles an hour. If the horse steps into an animal hole, its leg will snap like a stick broken over your knee. You'll probably get thrown and badly hurt. The horse will have to be shot. It's not something I ever wanted to have happen to Blazer.

The other reason is the horse. I've seen movies where the good guys chase the bad guys on horses, and it goes on and on and on and on. Like a car chase. When I see that, I get grumpy because it could never happen that way in real life. The longest you could ever keep a horse at full gallop is fifteen minutes. And if you pushed the horse that hard, its heart might actually explode. Horses aren't machines. They are athletes and can only be pushed so hard.

"I see you know how to ride," Stephanie said as she reined to a stop beside me.

"Just having fun," I said. To change the subject away from me, I pointed down the valley. "Ten minutes down that trail is where we found Big Boy."

Stephanie looked around. "No road. You were right. Whoever killed your cattle would have a tough time getting down there. Any ideas yet? Besides witches on broomsticks?"

"None," I said.

"You told me that the police only found footprints around the dead cattle. No tracks in. No tracks out. Right?"

"Right." I kept my horse moving alongside hers.

"Just like at our ranch," she said. She looked back toward the ranch house. "And just like at our ranch, the house is fairly far from where the cattle were killed but close enough that someone would have heard a helicopter in the distance. Maybe it *was* broomsticks."

I enjoyed watching the expressions on her face as she talked. It caught me by surprise when her eyes opened wide and her mouth formed an O of surprise.

"What?" I said.

"Ernest," she said. "It's been bugging me. I just remembered where I've seen him before. He was part of a work crew that built a new barn on our ranch."

"And?" I said.

"Don't you think it's strange he showed up here to work for you?"

"Guys like him move around a lot," I said. "You know that."

"Yes, I do. But here's something you don't know. We finished the new barn just after Champion and the rest of the cattle were killed on our ranch."

"Stephanie—"

"Look," she said, "he was at your ranch when your bull was killed. What does that tell you?"

"That maybe your dad is right about your imagination. You're not helping us come up with answers. You're just making the questions harder."

"At least," she said, "someone is asking questions."

Twelve

We reached the corral where the cattle had been killed. Dull brown smears still covered some of the grass and bushes. Dried blood. Looking at it, I remembered how angry Dad and I were when we first saw the dead cattle here.

"You've got that look on your face," Stephanie said.

"What look?"

"The one I've seen at hockey games. Sometimes you take your helmet off when you're sitting on the bench. When the Blazers are losing, you look mad and ready to take on the world."

"Oh."

She got off her horse and tied the reins to a tree branch. "Come on," she said. "Let's start walking circles, bigger and bigger until it's nearly dark. If you see anything, holler."

I did as she said. Although I was looking at the ground

as I walked, part of me was happy and grinning. *Stephanie had been watching me at hockey games . . .*

I started to daydream about scoring five goals in a playoff game. With her in the stands, of course. Then I figured if I was going to daydream, I might as well make it a good one. I'd score five goals, all right, but only after someone hit me so hard in the first period that my ribs were cracked.

Yes, that was it, I told myself as I reworked my daydream. I'd be a hero. Broken bones and still able to carry the team to victory. Then after the game she would give me a hug. I would manfully tell her it didn't hurt that much when she squeezed me. Then she would see the tears of pain in my eyes and admire me for being able to take all that pain in silence. She would look into my eyes. She would close her eyes and wait for me to kiss her. . . .

"Ouch!" I said. I began to hop up and down, holding my right foot with both hands. "Ouch! Ouch! Ouch!"

Stephanie came running over. "What is it?"

She didn't ask if it was a rattlesnake. It was too early in the year for rattlesnakes to be out of their dens.

"Ouch! Ouch! Ouch!" I said, still hopping on one foot. "It's my big toe."

I hopped around some more until my toe finally quit throbbing.

She giggled.

"What?" I said. I was cranky. "What are you laughing at?"

"You big baby. You were dancing like someone cut your foot off."

"Look," I said. "Cowboy boots don't have steel toes. I kicked something and . . ."

"Weren't you looking at the ground for clues? How come you didn't see where you were going?"

"Maybe, just for a second, I was thinking about something else, okay?" I walked back to the deep grass where I had whacked my foot against something hard. I bent over and moved the grass with my hands. I saw what I had kicked. "Why do you suppose there's a steel pole half buried in the ground?"

We both stared at it.

The pole was a little under knee height. It had been driven into the ground at an angle, like a giant tent peg. The top of the steel pole looped into a tight circle.

"It's like something to tie a rope to," Stephanie said.

I pulled at it. "It's stuck pretty tight."

Stephanie kneeled down. She stared at the top of the pole for a few minutes.

"Josh," she said, "with something this heavy, you would have to drive it into the ground with a sledge-hammer, right?"

"Unless you were tough like me," I said. "Then you could use your bare hands."

"Remember I just saw you hopping around and howling." She smiled. "But seriously . . ."

"Seriously," I said. "I agree. You'd need a sledge-hammer."

"Take a close look at how shiny the top is."

I looked. The dark steel was shiny where it had been flattened by a big hammer. "That only proves what we already knew," I said. "Someone drove this in with a big hammer."

"It also proves something else. Tell me *when* someone drove it in with the hammer."

It hit me. *A shiny spot where the steel had been dented.*

"It's only been here a short time," I said. "Otherwise the shiny part would have started to rust."

"Exactly," she said. "I think we can guess this has something to do with the night that Big Boy was killed."

"Any other guesses?"

"No," she answered. "Why would someone have tied a rope to this?"

We couldn't think of an answer. We didn't find anything else that was strange or out of place.

When we got back to the ranch house, Mom and Dad still weren't back from town. I needed to get to Kamloops to study for classes the next day, so we unsaddled the horses as fast as possible. We brushed them down and led them to their stalls in the barn.

Finally, we got to Stephanie's Bronco.

There was a note beneath her windshield wiper.

She opened it.

"Stay away," she said, reading from the note. "Or you will die like Big Boy."

Thirteen

Speaking of the war of 1812, here's some trivia for you," Mr. Robertson said at the front of the classroom. "Remember, it was Canada and the British against the United States of America."

Mr. Robertson was tall and wore a tweed sports jacket. He smoked a pipe, which he kept in his jacket pocket. He liked to pretend he was a university professor instead of a high school social studies teacher. In fact, most of us knew we would get graded easier if we called him Professor Robertson.

He wasn't a bad teacher. He tried to make things interesting for us.

"The British fleet actually moved so far up the river into Washington, D.C., that they nearly burned down the White House," he said. "That's how it got its name. The Americans used white paint to cover the soot and smoke."

Normally, I would have listened harder to Mr. Robertson. But my thoughts kept going back to the night before. After finding the threatening note, Stephanie had insisted we talk to Ernest.

Only trouble was, Ernest wasn't in the bunkhouse where the ranch hands stayed. Neither were any of his clothes. Ernest had vanished. That only added more questions to all of this.

Big Boy was dead. Stephanie's Champion was dead. Two other bulls of Locomotive's bloodline were dead. Who was killing cattle? Why? And what did Ernest have to do with any of it?

I glanced at the clock. Eleven fifty-three. Seven minutes to the end of class.

"Furthermore," Mr. Robertson was saying, "the American national anthem, 'The Star-Spangled Banner,' starts 'O say can you see, by the dawn's early light, what so proudly we hail'd at the twilight's last gleaming?' The writer, Francis Scott Key, was referring to the American flag. He had watched from a ship through the entire night of the British invasion. He thought the American flag would *not* be standing at dawn. Still, against overwhelming odds—"

"THESE ARE TODAY'S ANNOUNCEMENTS," the intercom interrupted. "ANNOUNCEMENT ONE: JOSH ELLROY IS REQUESTED TO REPORT TO THE OFFICE AT NOON. ANNOUNCEMENT TWO: INTRA-MURAL BADMINTON WINNERS ARE . . ."

I didn't hear the rest. I'd never been called to the office before. Was I in trouble? Had an emergency happened at the ranch?

As soon as the bell rang, I hurried to the office. The

secretary handed me a message. I read it once. I read it again.

Then I ran to a pay phone down the hall.

Fourteen

Dad," I said into the telephone, "glad I caught you at the house."

"Actually," he said, "I picked up the extension in the workshop."

I could picture where he was standing. The workshop was a big, heated building behind the barn. On a ranch as big as ours, there is a lot of equipment—trucks, tractors, and even a small bulldozer. We had a full-time mechanic who had plenty of repair work to keep him busy.

Dad would be standing at the front of the building, near the large tool bench. The old-fashioned, black telephone had a dial instead of numbers to punch.

"Where are you?" he asked. "I hear strange noises in the background."

"At school." The strange noises were the regular sounds of students laughing and talking as they moved down the hallway.

"I'm sorry you wasted a quarter to call," he said. "We

don't know much more than we did last night. There's still no sign of Ernest. Lloyd says he didn't even collect the pay we owe him."

Lloyd is the ranch foreman. Dad lets him do most of the hiring.

"But I've got our accountant trying to find out more about Ernest," Dad said.

Despite my news, I was curious. Last night, Dad had agreed Ernest might have had something to do with Big Boy's death. Dad had promised to let me know what he could find out about the man.

"Accountant?" I asked.

"Not too many people can get through modern life without leaving a paper trail," Dad said. "Credit reports, charge cards, all that stuff. An experienced money person can find out just as much about a person as a detective."

He paused. "By the way, hang on to your quarters. I promise, as soon as I learn anything, I'll call you."

"Dad . . . that's not why I called," I said.

"Is everything okay? You haven't gotten into a car accident, have you?"

I laughed. "Am I speaking to my mom?"

"Very funny. So why did you call?"

"Coach Price left me a message," I said. I took a deep breath. "I called him. He told me the Buffalo Sabres want me to play a few games with them in the National Hockey League."

"What!" He sounded like we had just won a lottery.

I felt the same way.

"It's true," I said. The Buffalo Sabres had drafted me at the end of last season. Because I was having such a good season, they had called Coach Price this morning. "The Sabres have a good lead in the race for the play-offs right now, and they want to give me a couple of games of NHL experience."

Dad gave a rodeo yell into the telephone.

I wanted to do the same back. But there were too many kids in the hallway.

"I'm proud of you, Josh. When?"

"Saturday. They're going to fly me from Vancouver to Los Angeles Saturday morning for the game against the Kings."

"This Saturday?" he asked.

"This Saturday," I said. "The day after tomorrow. It's part of their road trip to the West Coast. Sunday is a day off. On Monday, I'll play with them against the San Jose Sharks in a televised game."

Another rodeo yell. "That's great news," he said. "Wait till I tell the boys out here."

"Thanks, Dad," I said. "Do you want to tell Mom? Or should I?"

"You. Call tonight. I'll do my best to keep it a secret so you can surprise her. And by then maybe I'll know more about Ernest."

He chuckled. "I love it. Saturday night you'll be playing in the NHL. Think you can take good care of yourself until then?"

"I sure do," I said. Of course, at that moment, I didn't know what Stephanie Becker had learned.

Fifteen

Regular afternoon practice did not seem like regular afternoon practice. Besides my dad, I'd only told Gordie Penn about my chance to play in the NHL. From him, though, the news had spread like fire through dry grass.

As I walked into the dressing room, guys high-fived me. Others slapped my back. It nearly brought me to tears, seeing how happy they were for me.

Luke Zannetti, though, made a point of keeping his head down as he got into his hockey gear. It made me sad, in a way. I hoped I would have been glad to see him get a chance to play with the Montreal Canadians. We were both on the same team. We had both been drafted into the NHL. I didn't think we had a reason to be jealous of each other.

I sat at my bench and pulled off my cowboy boots. I leaned back and listened to the chatter of the dressing room. Then I got nervous thinking about my first NHL game.

Here, at least, I knew I fit in. These guys were my friends. With the Buffalo Sabres, I'd just be a kid among strangers. Then I thought it was weird that just as my dreams were coming true, I was afraid of them. In my mind, I gave myself a kick and told myself to stop worrying.

Five minutes later, I was on the ice, skating in circles to warm up.

Five minutes after that, we were in the middle of a three-on-two passing drill, where three forwards rushed down the ice and tried to score on two defensemen. One winger cut to the net. The other winger dropped back to split the defense. And the center decided to pass or shoot.

Coach Price had kept Luke and me on the same line. In five rushes, Luke had passed four times to the other winger and had taken one shot. His moves, of course, were his decisions. But three times I'd been so wide open for a pass that I could have taken a nap after getting the puck and still had enough time to score.

It didn't surprise me on the next rush when Luke lifted his stick to take a slap shot* instead of passing to me. I was wide open—again—but I'd figured out Luke was doing his best to ignore me. I wasn't going to let him think I cared. I kept skating hard, telling myself all I could do was my best. If I started worrying about Luke, I would be giving him power over me.

Luke snapped his stick downward. Only as he was taking the monster slap shot, he turned his hips and shoulders and aimed at me instead of the net.

The puck rifled at my head. Bang! It dinged my helmet just above my ear. I fell sideways and slammed to the ice. For a second, all I saw was black. I blinked a few times, and all I saw was white. I realized I was staring at the ice right beneath my nose.

I groaned and pushed myself back to my feet. I staggered over toward Luke. Some of the guys moved away, expecting a fight. Coach Price, at the other end of the rink, started skating toward us.

"That's twice," I said. It's one thing to be a team player. It's another to let someone push you around. "If there's a third time, I'm coming after you. I won't even stop to warn you. I'm just going to take you down."

Luke's reply?

He switched grips on his hockey stick. Holding it like a bat, he swung downward with full force against my leg. His stick broke across the side of my thigh.

I jumped him.

He fell backward.

I brought my fist back to hammer him.

Someone grabbed my arm.

"Enough!" It was Coach Price. He was roaring with anger. "Enough!"

I allowed him to pull me away from Luke.

Luke got to his feet and stared anger at me. Neither of us said anything.

Coach Price got between us.

"Guys," he said to the rest of the team, "five-minute break. Go for a light skate."

The other players slowly skated away.

"What is wrong with you two?" Coach Price asked. "This isn't kindergarten. You're nearly grown men."

I opened my mouth to tell him that Luke had started it. Then I realized I would sound just like a five-year-old. So I snapped my mouth shut. If Coach Price hadn't figured out what had happened, he wasn't going to listen to me anyway.

Luke didn't say anything either. He just stared at me, breathing heavy.

"This is a Memorial Cup team," Coach Price said, "not a Mickey Mouse outfit with no discipline. You're my two best players. I need you. But nobody needs you bad enough to let you get away with this and wreck the rest of the team."

Coach Price waited for either of us to speak. He got more silence.

"Here's the deal," he finally said. "Tonight, you two are going to meet somewhere. I don't care where. I don't care when. But you're going to sit down and talk through whatever is eating at you both."

"Coach, I—" Luke began.

"Cork it, Luke. Listen or leave the ice right now. If you leave, don't come back."

By Luke's face, I could tell he wanted to speak. But he held back.

"Like I said, talk it through," Coach said. "Without me. I'm not a babysitter. Understand?"

Coach Price barked at me. "Ellroy. When? Where?"

"McDonald's," I said, after a few seconds. This wasn't fair. It wasn't my fault. But Coach was right. If

63

we didn't solve it, it would hurt the team. "The one down by the river. Six o'clock."

"You heard him, Zannetti? You'll be there?"

Luke nodded.

"Good," Coach Price said. "If you don't get this stupidity straightened out, you're both off the team. And both of you remember, if you're not part of the Blazers, you're going to have a real tough time getting into the NHL."

Coach Price gave me one last look.

"Which means, Ellroy," he said, "if you two don't solve this, no trip for you to California this weekend to play for the Sabres."

Sixteen

I sure didn't need more pressure as I walked through the McDonald's parking lot to meet Luke at six o'clock. But there was a note in my back pocket. It had been under my windshield wiper when I left the Riverside Coliseum at the end of practice.

Josh, I made some more calls today. There is another rancher who might be able to help us. I've got some other things to do, so I can't wait for you right now. I know you don't have a game tonight, so I hope you can meet me at 6:30. Take the Logan Lake exit off the Coke until it hits 97C south. I'll be waiting at that intersection. We'll talk to the rancher together. It's important.

x o x o x o—Steph

On the bottom of the page, she had drawn a map for me. The Coke was short for the Coquihalla Highway, which went south from Kamloops to Vancouver. The

Logan Lake exit was about a twenty-minute drive from Kamloops. From there, I was to go west for about another fifteen minutes to reach Highway 97C where it turned south to Merritt.

The part I liked best about the note was the xs and os where she signed her name. I was pretty sure that meant "hugs and kisses."

The part I didn't like was the time pressure. It was more than half an hour to there from the McDonald's. There was no way to reach Stephanie and let her know about my meeting with Luke. But if I didn't meet with Luke, I was off the team. And if I was off the team, I wouldn't be able to play in the NHL this weekend.

I could think of only one solution.

I pushed through the door into the usual noise of kids and lines at McDonald's. I looked for Luke.

No Luke. Plenty of other people and a big poster of Ronald McDonald. But no Luke.

I looked at my watch. Six o'clock.

At ten minutes after six, still no Luke. Even if I left now, I'd be ten or fifteen minutes late to meet Stephanie. I wondered what she had talked about with the rancher. I wondered if she would wait for me.

I ordered and drank a chocolate milkshake.

Twenty minutes after six. Still no Luke.

I ordered and drank another chocolate milkshake. Just as I was throwing the cup into the garbage, Luke walked in, wearing his Kamloops Blazers team jacket.

I didn't look at my watch. I didn't have to. I knew it

was 6:30 because I'd been looking at my watch every thirty seconds.

I had a choice. I could say something to him about making me wait. Or I could smile through my anger. Saying something to him would just make him defensive, and it wouldn't change the fact that he was late. So, instead, I smiled.

"Hey, Luke," I said.

"Whatever," he said. No smile.

I noticed he was wearing a baseball cap. If he thought it was cool to be bald like Michael Jordan, why was he covering his shaved head?

I didn't ask him that, though. I kept smiling. I needed a favor from him. The best I'd be able to do was meet Stephanie some time after seven o'clock. And only if Luke helped.

"I know Coach Price wants us to talk," I said. "Any chance we can do it while I'm driving?"

"Where? Why?" he asked.

I explained as much as I could.

"Bloodlines and dead cows?" he said. "Forget it. And don't expect us to talk this through either. I just came down here to tell you I don't care whether we play for the team or not."

Something inside me snapped. This was the guy who had punched me. This was the guy who might cost me a trip to the NHL. This was the guy who now smirked at me because he was happy to be able to say no and make life difficult for me.

I grabbed the front of his jacket with both hands. I

yanked him toward me. I lifted him onto his tiptoes, surprised that he was lighter than I had expected.

We were in our own private world among all the people around us.

"Look," I whispered between gritted teeth. "I'm about to stomp you good. We both know this is your fault. So if I'm going to go down anyway, I might as well make you pay."

Then I realized what I was doing. I was threatening to beat someone up. When I was fourteen, I'd gotten into a fight at school. I'd expected Dad to punish me for it. Talking to me later, though, Dad had not gotten angry at me; he'd been sad. He'd said that God had seen fit to put my soul into a body built stronger and faster than most others. It was not something to take pride in; it was simply the way I'd been born. He'd said it was a shame to take that gift and use it to hurt others. He'd also said that violence is something that stupid people do because they can't think of better solutions. Then Dad had walked out of my room and left me to think.

I let go of Luke's jacket.

"I'm sorry," I said. "That wasn't right. I just wish I knew what's going through your head."

Luke stared at me for a few seconds. Shaved skull. Dark eyebrows. Dark eyes. He bit his lower lip.

"You should have hit me," he finally said. "I really don't care about anything. And I wanted to be able to hate you."

His eyes got shiny. He turned his head away from me and started walking to the door.

"Come on," he said, without looking back. "Let's get in that stupid truck of yours."

I wasn't sure. But it sounded like he had started to cry.

Seventeen

Luke didn't say anything as I pulled out of the parking lot. It was dark, but as we passed beneath a street light, I looked over. His face was turned away from me. He was leaning against the passenger door, the bill of his baseball cap pressed against the window.

I didn't know what to say either. Coach Price had told us to talk it through. I had no idea what *it* was. Until a few minutes earlier, I hadn't even known that Luke wanted to hate me. I couldn't figure out why. I'd never done anything to him.

We traveled through town in silence. The highway climbed the mountain and the lights of the city glowed below us. With the radio off, there was only the hum of tires and the whistle of wind against the speeding truck.

I waited until we were on the Coquihalla Highway to speak.

"Is it because I got the MVP last year?" I asked. It was the only thing I could figure.

"Huh?" My voice had made him jump, like his mind was a million miles away.

"Is that why you want to hate me?" I asked. "Is it because you didn't win the MVP?"

He laughed. It was a bitter sound. "I didn't like it. But you deserved it. I might have been a better hockey player. But you helped the team more. Even I have to admit that."

"Oh," I said. *He'd just said he might have been a better hockey player. Like he wasn't any more.*

"Do you hate me because you're in a slump?" I'd said it. I'd put it out in the open. Said what the guys were saying behind his back.

"I said I *wanted* to hate you. And yes, that's part of it."

He sighed, loud enough to be heard above the wind noise. On both sides of the highway, the pine trees were dark outlines, like soldiers guarding the land.

"You're nice," he said. "You go to church. You smile all the time. You don't get mad at things. Even if you couldn't play good hockey, people would like being around you. Me?"

There was some silence before he started again.

"Me. I always had hockey. Now it's going away. It's not fun to watch you get better and better *and* have people like you."

"What do you mean," I asked slowly, "about your hockey going away?"

He turned away again, a movement I caught out of the corner of my eye.

"I'm real messed up, okay? Let's leave it at that."

Messed up? I thought of how badly he had been playing. I thought of how slow and weak he had been on the ice. I thought of how light he had felt when I grabbed him by the jacket.

Messed up? I didn't know much about drugs, but I had to wonder if that's what he meant.

"You can get help," I said, thinking if he wanted to explain, he would.

"Tell you what," he said. "Let's not talk anymore."

"But Coach Price—"

"Yeah, yeah. Coach Price. Tomorrow, go ahead and tell him we talked it through. Tell him everything will be fine. And it will be. I promise I won't give you any trouble. In McDonald's, I found out I don't have the energy to hate you."

He paused. His voice got a little stronger, as if he were grinning. "No, I changed my mind. I want to make a deal with you. Help me get through the season, and I'll stop pushing you."

"Help you get through the season?" I repeated, confused.

"Be a friend. Stick up for me. I can't tell you how much I hate it when the guys bug me about my shaved head."

"Then why did you—"

"Look, just make the deal."

"Sure," I said. He shouldn't have had to ask. We were on the same team.

"Good. Now get us to this meeting with your girlfriend."

Girlfriend. I liked the sound of that.

"I'll sit in the truck and shut up," he finished. "You won't even know I'm around."

Trouble was, when we got there, Stephanie wasn't around either.

Eighteen

The headlights of my truck picked up a pile of rocks beside the stop sign. Had someone stacked them there? Stephanie?

I let the truck idle and got out. A night breeze chilled me. The stars above were white dust in a black, black sky. The hills were dark. It was a lonely highway. It was a lonely intersection.

The final rock on top of the pile held down a piece of paper.

I grinned. Stephanie was pretty smart. I pulled out the paper and took it back to the truck. I switched on the dash light.

"What is it?" Luke asked.

I read it out loud, skipping the hugs and kisses part at the bottom. "Sorry we missed each other. Hope you are just late. If you get here by 7:30, go to the Belkie ranch. (Dan Belkie.) I should be there at least that long. Steph."

It was ten past seven. We had lots of time.

Again, she had drawn a map with the note. I handed the map to Luke and left the dash light on as I started to drive.

"Read out the directions as I drive," I said.

"Hugs and kisses?" he asked, reading the bottom of the note.

"Yeah, yeah." In my hurry, I'd forgotten it was there in her neat handwriting. "Just read the directions, will ya?"

The driveway to the Belkie ranch was off a gravel road, well up a hill, about fifteen miles from the intersection. As the headlights swept through the turn, I saw the entrance was marked by old wagon wheels and a large mailbox.

Gravel and rocks bounced off the bottom of the truck. The drive up to the ranch was narrow and twisted its way up the steep hill. Maybe I was going a little fast, especially for that kind of road. But it was a long way to the ranch house, and I wanted to get there soon. For some reason, I was nervous. Maybe because this ranch was so far away from any town. Maybe because of the black night. Maybe because I had no idea what was happening.

There was a light on in the kitchen of the ranch house. It was a long, low house with a sidewalk that lead from the drive to the front door.

I parked the truck. Luke waited inside.

A Border collie ran up to me as I stepped out. It sniffed at my pant legs. I scratched between its ears. Most farm dogs go crazy when strangers arrive. Not this one. It was friendly and followed me up the sidewalk. A single yard light threw a shadow ahead of me as I walked.

I rang the doorbell. No one answered. I rang again. Still no answer.

I walked back to the truck and opened the door.

"Weird," I said to Luke, standing outside. "She should be here. We didn't see anyone come back out on the road."

"Unless her directions were bad. She is a girl."

He caught the look on my face. "Bad joke?"

"Yup," I said. "You mind waiting? I'm going to look around."

"Don't have much else to do," he said, slouching back against the seat. He was sounding almost human.

I walked away from the house toward the barn, which was a couple hundred yards away. As I walked farther from the house, it got darker and darker. The collie stayed with me, running little circles.

I heard the low moaning of cattle in pens on the other side of the barn. As I got closer, I heard voices.

Just as I reached the barn, an outside light switched on. I jumped. Then I saw that it was a security light rigged to go on when it senses movement.

The light showed a set of wide barn doors, half open.

"Hello?" I called out as I walked up to the doors. "Hello?"

I didn't want anyone to think I was sneaking around.

I peeked inside. A big man in coveralls stepped toward me. I jumped again.

"Hello," I said. "Are you Dan Belkie?"

"Long ways from the beaten path, son," the man said. He had wild, bushy hair. His hands and wrists stuck out a couple of inches from his shirt sleeves. He wore big work boots.

"I'm sorry to bother you," I said. "I have a friend named Stephanie Becker. She told me to meet her here. She was going to talk to Dan Belkie."

Another man joined us. He was much smaller than the wild-haired guy. He wore tan pants and a sweater. "I'm Dan Belkie. This is my foreman, Jim Cowle."

"Yes, sir," I said. "My name is Josh Ellroy."

I stuck out my hand. Dan Belkie stepped forward and shook it. The big man didn't.

"Ellroy," he said. "As in Ryan Ellroy?"

"Yes, sir. He's my father."

"And quite the rancher. Pleased to meet you. What can I help you with? You were talking about a girl?"

"She told me she was coming here to meet you. Have you seen her?"

The big man quietly moved around behind me. I didn't like that. But it seemed rude to say anything. What was he going to do? Jump me? Dumb thought. Even so, the skin on my neck prickled.

"Haven't seen any girl," Dan Belkie said. His voice was soft. It sounded educated, with an English accent. "You say her name was Stephanie?"

"Yes." I looked past Dan Belkie. With the big man out of the doorway, I could see a little more of the inside of the barn. I saw the bed of a pickup truck. In it was a large basket, big enough for two or three people to stand inside. Some ropes hung over the side of the basket.

"Maybe she's playing a joke on you," Belkie said. "It's a shame you had to drive all the way out here by yourself."

"Actually," I said as I jerked a thumb back over my shoulder at my parked truck, "I have a friend with me."

"Oh." Belkie shook his head. For a second, it seemed like he was looking at the big man behind me. "Well, then at least you'll have company on your way back."

"You're sure," I said, "that Stephanie never made it here?"

"Young man, are you accusing me of lying?"

I felt my ears turn red. "I didn't mean it that way. It's just that . . ."

I stopped. If he was lying, I wouldn't get anywhere like this. If he wasn't lying, I would just be making a fool of myself.

"It must be a joke," I said. "Stephanie lives on a ranch too. She's probably with her friends right now, killing herself with laughter."

Dan Belkie put his hand on my shoulder and guided me back toward the house. We walked side by side. When I headed back to my truck, he dropped his hand.

I can take a hint. He wanted me to leave.

"Well, sir," I said as we reached the truck, "I'm sorry to have bothered you."

"No bother," he said. "Have a safe drive back. These mountain roads can be dangerous."

I felt a chill run through me. And it wasn't from the cold mountain air. It was from the way he said it.

Nineteen

What's going on?" Luke asked.

I didn't answer until I had driven out of the ranch yard and we were on the long drive back to the main road.

"Weird stuff," I said. "They told me that Stephanie never made it there."

"Maybe she changed her mind," Luke said.

"Maybe." Luke had not been there at the doorway to know how strange it had been. The men had seemed like hunters, eyeing me as if I were a deer in their gunsights.

I thought of the pickup truck inside the barn. "Luke, what would you do with a basket big enough to hold three people?"

"Is this a riddle?"

"No." I described what I had seen.

"Oh," he said. "It's probably from a hot-air balloon. Especially if it's in the back of a truck."

"Hot-air balloon?"

"My parents took me for a ride in one as a present on my sixteenth birthday. The guys who pilot the balloon need a way to get the balloon to and from their launch site. They load the basket in the truck. Plus the empty, folded up balloon. Plus the gas burner."

I was driving slowly because my mind was working on something.

"Burner," I repeated to myself out loud.

"Yeah. Burner," Luke said, thinking I had asked a question. "They need to heat the air to fill the balloon. That was the cool part. Watching the balloon fill until it lifted the basket into the air. If they hadn't tied it down with ropes, it would have just floated away without us."

"Ropes." Sure. There had been ropes tied to the basket. *Why was that bugging me?*

"What a noise, though," Luke said. "That burner really roars. The balloon ride is really quiet, except when the pilot turns the burner on to lift it some more."

"Noise," I said. That was bugging me too.

"Lots of noise. I was watching the burner, thinking it would be great to roast some hot dogs over the flame."

"Flame." I must have sounded like an idiot to Luke.

Then I put it together. Rope. Burner. Noise. Flame.

Without warning, I swung the truck's steering wheel hard. We bounced off the road, down through a small ditch, and up the other side.

"What are you doing?!" Luke said.

I ignored him. I wrestled the steering wheel and managed to get the truck between the trees. I drove a little farther until we were well off the road.

I put the truck in park and turned off the ignition. I also shut the headlights off.

"I'm going to ask you again," Luke said. "What are you doing?"

"Broomsticks," I told him. I reached across him to the glove box of the truck. Ranchers always carried flashlights. I would need mine. "We have to go back to the ranch. On foot."

"Try making sense," he said.

I grabbed the flashlight from the glove box. I stepped out of the truck. Luke got out too. We stood there in the mountain darkness. The truck engine ticked as it cooled down.

"Broomsticks," I repeated. I was about to explain when I heard a new sound.

"Listen," I said. "What's that?"

Luke listened. "Sounds like a car or truck. It's coming from the ranch."

"Maybe it's Stephanie." I began to walk among the trees toward the road, using the flashlight to show me a path. Luke followed me.

The sound of the vehicle got louder. I shut the flashlight off and stood beside a tree. I didn't have a good feeling about this. Especially since I didn't see headlights.

A minute later, I understood why. The truck was traveling without its lights on. As it passed us, I saw the outline of Jim Cowle, the big foreman, behind the steering wheel. He was hunched forward, peering at the road ahead of him.

"Spooky," Luke said. "Why not use headlights?"

"Maybe because he doesn't want to be seen."

"By who?" Luke asked. "The only other people on the road would be us. They know that because we just left."

"Exactly," I told him. "Let me ask you something. If you and I were in the truck right now, on that road, would we see him coming up behind us?"

"No."

"Does that tell you anything?"

"Yes," Luke said after a couple of seconds. "And I don't like it. What is going on here?"

"We're going to find out," I said, "by going back to the ranch. On foot. Remember?"

Twenty

As we got closer, I whispered to Luke that I wanted to go to the barn first. Of any of the buildings, it would be the easiest to get inside. We were looking for Stephanie or her Bronco 4 x 4. After that, I hoped to find something that would help me figure out more of this puzzle. If Stephanie wasn't in the barn, we'd go to the house next.

We circled around the house. Stopping in a stand of trees, we listened for any signs that someone knew we were around.

"We'll have to come up to the barn from behind," I whispered to Luke. "In front, there's a security light."

Luke pointed in the direction of the barn. Our eyes had adjusted to the night light, and we didn't need the flashlight. Not with the full moon that had risen.

"But there are animals back there," he whispered.

He was right, of course. There were pens and corrals with cattle. Not only could we see the dark outlines of the animals moving around, but we could also smell and hear them.

"Your point?" I asked.

"Big animals," he said. "With pointy horns . . ."

"Stay on the right side of the fence and the big animals can't get you." I grinned in the darkness. "Besides, you've faced plenty of big animals in hockey."

"I can't do it. It's like some people have a fear of heights. Me, it's this . . ." He let his voice trail away. I was already walking toward the pens behind the barn.

"Then wait at the truck," I said. I was worried enough already. The last thing I needed was to have to babysit him.

I left him behind. Near the back of the barn, I was able to get a sense of the layout of the pens and corrals. There were four big corrals, set up with dozens of cattle in each one. There were some smaller pens, with only a couple of animals. Ranchers sometimes separated cows with new calves from the rest of the herd.

I walked past the pens to the rear entrance of the barn. It was a much smaller door than the one at the front. It was also locked.

I looked upward. On the second floor of the barn, there was an opening. If it was anything like our barn, most of the second floor was hayloft, a place to store bales of hay. Workers would pitch hay down through the opening above.

I tucked the flashlight into the front of my shirt. I found some hay bales and stacked them on top of each other. The stack wobbled dangerously, but I was finally high enough to reach the opening with my fingers. I hooked on, pulled myself up, and wiggled my way into the hayloft.

Once I was on my feet again, I took the flashlight out of my shirt. Without the moonlight, it was almost black. I used the flashlight beam to find a set of wooden stairs down to the main level.

The front half of the barn was a wide-open work area. I swept my flashlight beam in all directions. I saw the pickup truck with the hot-air balloon basket. Behind it was a workbench with tools. Beside it was the fabric of the balloon. Next to the fabric was a gigantic leather strap. I couldn't figure out what it was for, so I moved on.

A door led to the back half of the barn. I pushed it open slowly and listened in the darkness. I heard rustling. It was a familiar rustling, the movement of animals in stalls.

I didn't want to waste time, so I moved inside quickly. There was a slight chance—if indeed they had Stephanie—that she was inside one of the stalls.

My flashlight showed stalls on both sides. The floor between was concrete, with a groove in the middle for water to run to a grate.

I stepped through the door. I shone my light into the first stall. Staring back at me was a monstrous bull. I moved on.

The next stall showed another bull. And another.

It was at the fourth stall that my heart rate doubled.

My flashlight beam clearly showed the animal inside.

It was another bull, all right, which shouldn't have surprised me. What did surprise me was one simple fact. The bull inside was Big Boy. Our bull. The one that had been chopped into pieces.

I had no doubt it was him. I'd worked with Big Boy for years. I knew every marking on his black hide. Just to be sure, I climbed the stall and aimed the flashlight beam at his side. Very clear in the light was the brand of the Ellroy ranch.

I climbed back down.

Big Boy? Here? Alive?

It was so unexpected, I felt like I'd been slammed in the head with another one of Luke's slap shots.

I took another step toward the next stall. Then I froze. The overhead lights had just been snapped on!

Before I could move, someone kicked the door behind me open.

"Turn around," came the soft voice with the English accent.

I turned, getting ready to charge him.

Dan Belkie stood in the doorway with a rifle leveled from his shoulder, pointing straight at me.

"Fool," he said. "Didn't you wonder why my dog isn't trained to bark at strangers? I don't need warning. Not with all the electronic devices I have—motion detectors and video cameras. As soon as you stepped into the barn, I knew."

"You've got our champion bull," I said.

"Not for long," Belkie said, smiling. "Tomorrow, all the bulls go by ship to Japan. Cowle radioed back to me. I already know your truck hasn't left the ranch. We'll find it and your friend. As for you and the stupid, stupid girl, you're both going to die in her 4 x 4."

I saw his finger tighten on the trigger. I heard a pppffft of air. Something slammed into my shoulder. I looked down at my jeans jacket. A dart was stuck hard into me, just below my collarbone.

I looked back at Dan Belkie. He was still smiling a broad, evil smile.

I dropped the flashlight and yanked the dart out.

Dan Belkie kept smiling. His face began to blur. The smile became like the nightmare smile of a monster as his face changed shape. Around him it got blacker and blacker. The black began to fill the whole room until, finally, it closed in on me.

There was a bang. My last thought was to dimly realize the bang was my head hitting concrete.

Everything ended.

Twenty-One

Josh? Josh?"

I groaned. My tongue felt like a wool sock sticking to the roof of my mouth.

"Josh?"

I managed to crack my eyes open. It took a few moments, but I could finally see that I was inside a Bronco. The windows were steamed.

"Josh?"

It hurt just to turn my head. "Stephanie?"

My voice was a ragged croak.

"Josh! I'm so glad you're awake."

My eyes began to focus. Stephanie sat beside me in her Bronco 4 x 4. Her wrists were taped to the steering wheel.

"My ankles are taped too," she said, answering my question before I could ask. "We're in one of the storage sheds at the back of the ranch."

I reached over for her. I discovered my wrists were

taped too. And my ankles. Just like Stephanie, I was bound with strips of wide, gray duct tape that is strong enough to keep furnace pipes together. A short rope tied my wrists to my ankles so that I could barely move my arms. Worse, my fingers had been taped together so I couldn't pull on the tape.

I swallowed a few times. "What . . . is . . . going . . . on?"

"He shot you with a tranquilizer gun. The same one he used on Champion, Big Boy, and the other bloodline bulls. He said you would be out for hours."

I managed to laugh. "I know how he shot me. I was there. I pulled the dart out."

It hurt too much to keep laughing. The rest of my words came out in a whisper. "What I meant was, why are you here? What's with the note? How did you know this was the ranch? And Big Boy, he's alive . . ."

She took a deep breath. "Today, I got to thinking. If four of Locomotive's bloodline had been killed already, wasn't there a good chance it would continue? Plus, if that Ernest guy had been at our ranch and your ranch, he'd probably show up at the next ranch where the killings would happen."

"Makes sense," I said. The clock on the dash showed 12:01. I'd been out of it about four hours.

"So I went back to the list of ranchers with a bull sired by Locomotive," she said. "I called them one by one. I first asked them if someone who looked like Ernest had ever showed up to ask for work. I also explained why I thought their bulls were in danger and told them to guard the animals."

"Still makes sense," I said. "But how did you get here, to the Belkie ranch?"

"Simple." She wriggled her fingers against the steering wheel and winced in pain. I understood. My own fingers were numb from the tight tape.

"Most of the other ranchers didn't sound like they believed me. But when I called here, Dan Belkie listened to my whole story. Then he said he might know something interesting that would help me. We set up a time to meet. I had a ton of errands to do in town, so I couldn't wait for you. You must have gotten both of my notes, otherwise you wouldn't be here."

I bent forward and tried to lift my hands to my mouth. Maybe I could bite through the tape. It didn't work. My head pressed against the dash, and my hands stopped just short of my teeth.

"Let me guess," I said as I sat back. "Belkie wanted to get you out here because he was worried you knew too much. You couldn't know, of course, that he was the one behind all this."

"He reeled me in like a fish," she said. "When I got here, I made the mistake of telling him you were the only person who knew where I had gone. So he and the other man moved the truck in here and tied me to the steering wheel. Then Belkie told me the rest."

"Hot-air balloon," I said. The gigantic leather harness that I'd seen in the barn now made sense. "They were rustling prize bulls using a hot-air balloon."

"He told you?"

"Nope." If it was the only thing I'd done right all day, I could at least feel good about figuring it out.

"Remember you told me that one of the ranch workers heard a roar and saw a glow in the sky, as if a UFO had landed?"

"In Montana," she said.

"Right. The roar must have been the burner they used to put hot air into the balloon. The glow came from the flame. And remember the steel rod I accidentally kicked at my ranch? They must have used it to tie a rope to the balloon so it wouldn't float away while they were killing the cattle. I'm guessing they used a few steel rods. The one we found was too hard to pull, so they left it behind."

Stephanie smiled. "I admit, I'm impressed. And here I thought you were just a handsome face."

I didn't know if she was serious or not. So I kept speaking as if I hadn't heard.

"They would lift out the prize bulls with the balloon, wouldn't they?"

"You saw the harness. I think they're getting ready to do some more rustling."

"It's a great idea," I said. "No helicopter, no airplane, no trucks. Almost like swooping in on a broomstick."

Stephanie nodded and told me what she'd learned from Dan Belkie. Ernest would find work at the ranch with the prize bull. He'd wait until he knew a good time to steal the bull. Belkie and the big guy would drive as close as possible with the truck, making sure to find a place where the wind would cause them to drift toward the cattle. Ernest would signal them with a flashlight, guiding them to the exact spot.

They used the balloon to carry in a bull about the same size and color as the prize bull. When they landed, they would tranquilize all the cattle they planned to kill. Once the prize bull was tranquilized and harnessed, they would kill all the other cattle, chopping them up so it looked like a cult killing. Their main goal, though, was to chop up the bull they had brought in, so no one could tell they'd made a switch. That way, if it looked like the prize bull was dead, no one would ever go looking for it.

"Hang on," I said, stopping her. "Big Boy is worth a lot of money. But only if he can be used for stud services. If a rancher doesn't know he's Big Boy, the rancher won't pay expensive stud fees."

"That's what I said too. If you can't advertise the bloodline, you can't sell stud fees."

"And?" I asked.

"Belkie had one of his own bulls sired by Locomotive. With Big Boy, Champion, and the two bulls from Montana and Alberta, he now has five of the bloodline. He wants to make money in two ways. First of all, with the other bulls off the market, it makes his worth more. He can raise his stud fees if people don't have the other bulls to go to."

She was right, which made me angrier.

"He'll sell the others," she said. "Far away from here, where it's unlikely any rancher will ever recognize them. Someone in Japan wants to start a new herd using the other four bulls."

"It sounds like he's got it all figured out."

She didn't say anything for a few minutes. The dashboard clock moved to 12:14. Then 12:15.

"Steph?" *Why had she stopped talking?*

"He's got it figured out, Josh. Including how you and I are going to die."

Twenty-Two

Tell me," I said as softly as I could. "How are they going to kill us?"

"Carbon monoxide. They're going to take my truck to the end of some road. Then they're going to rig a hose from the exhaust pipe into the window and let the motor run. When we're dead, they'll pull the hose out and untape us. It'll look like a couple of teenagers who wanted to be alone accidentally died while sitting in a parked truck with the motor running."

"Great," I said.

"You're not scared?"

"Of course I am," I said. "But I'm not going to give up. Maybe I can lean over and pull the tape off your hands with my teeth."

I tilted in her direction.

"Josh?"

"Yes?" I was looking into her eyes from only a couple of inches away.

"*I'm* scared. Will you kiss me?"

I leaned as close as I could. She leaned my way. Our lips got closer and closer.

"Um, Steph?"

"Yes?"

"This is as far as I can stretch."

"Me too."

There we were, so close I could feel her breath. Yet so far apart I'd never be able to kiss her before I died.

Talk about rotten luck.

Then Luke knocked on the windshield.

"Hey, guys," he said. "Am I interrupting anything?"

Five minutes later, we were free, standing in the near darkness of the storage shed. The moonlight coming through a small window showed bags of feed stacked against the walls around Stephanie's 4 x 4.

"What happened?" I asked. "I thought you were going to wait back at the truck?"

"I saw the Belkie guy leave his house with a rifle. I couldn't just walk out on you. Then I saw them drag you out of the barn. I followed them, so I knew where you were all the time."

"All the time?" I said. Four hours had passed.

"They heard me outside," Luke said. He looked at his feet. "I had to hide. Then I watched the shed for a long time to make sure it was safe to come in."

"Where did you hide?" Stephanie asked.

He kept his head down. His voice was shaky. "I went into the cattle pens. They had this stupid dog, and I was afraid it would smell me unless I was around all those animals."

"Big animals," I said. "With pointy horns. Remember?"

He shrugged like it was no big deal. I knew it was.

I rubbed his bald head like I was trying to shine it. "You're a stand-up guy, Luke. Thanks."

"We should go," Stephanie said. "They might come back."

Luke started for the door with Stephanie behind him. I followed them out after getting a flashlight I'd spotted in Stephanie's 4 x 4.

"If we can make it to my truck," I said, "we'll have a real good shot at escaping. But let's go the long away around."

We stepped into the crisp air. We half jogged away from the ranch house and barn and animal pens.

We were five minutes away when I stopped so suddenly that Luke ran into my back.

"What is it?" he asked.

"Guys," I said. "You go on without me."

"I don't get it," Stephanie said. "Where are you going?"

My breath blew out in white puffs as I spoke. "How long before they find out we're gone? Half an hour? One hour? Two hours?"

"What does it matter?" Luke said. "We'll reach Kamloops by then. The police will be on their way back here."

"Exactly," I said. "Police. That's what they'll be thinking when they don't find us."

"And?" Luke asked.

"And they'll do the one thing they can to save themselves. They'll get rid of the four prize bulls in the barn. That way, no one can prove anything against them."

"He's right," Stephanie said.

"He's crazy," Luke said to her. "What's Josh going to do, go back to the barn and let the bulls out?"

"Yup," I said. "You two get to the truck and take off. Call the police from the first pay phone you find. Once the bulls are out, I'll hide somewhere until the police get here."

"You can't do that," Luke said. "If those two guys catch you, they'll kill you."

"If I don't do it," I said, "they're going to kill hundreds of thousands of dollars' worth of bloodline bulls. Including the one I used to feed by hand with a bottle."

I turned and ran back toward the barn.

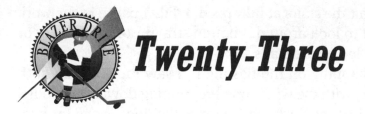

Twenty-Three

I hadn't told Luke and Stephanie about the motion detectors and video cameras in the barn because I didn't want to scare them. I was already scared enough for the three of us.

I did have a plan, though.

I knew as soon as I stepped into the barn, there was a good chance Belkie would know I was there. Since I didn't have the time or skill to find a way around the alarms he had rigged, I wasn't even going to bother trying. Instead, I would try a hit-and-run. And it would have to be a fast hit-and-run.

When I got to the dark shadows behind the barn, I didn't waste a second. The hay bales were still where I had piled them earlier. I jumped up, reached for the hayloft opening, and pulled myself inside.

I ran across the hayloft toward the wooden stairs. There were no lights on in the work area below, so I knew it was safe to go downstairs. At least, safe for now.

I hit the stairs at full speed. I didn't pause in the work area to look around. I bolted straight toward the door that led to the stalls.

Snapping on the flashlight, I saw the stalls on both sides, with the wide concrete running down the middle. I flicked the flashlight beam at the door at the far end. Just outside of that locked door were the cattle pens and wide open hills. The bulls would be safe there. We could always round them up later.

I dashed toward the rear door. Had Belkie already heard the alarms? Was he or the big, ugly man named Cowle already on the way with a rifle?

At the rear door, I skidded to a stop.

My flashlight told me what I didn't want to know. The lock was not a bolt you turned by hand. It needed a key.

I turned and ran back to the work area. It took me nearly half a minute, but I finally spotted a hammer. I picked it up and ran back to the rear door of the barn.

Bang! Bang!

If an alarm had not gotten their attention, the hammering would.

Bang! Bang! Bang!

I was desperate. There was no turning back for me. Belkie had to be on his way. He would be coming from the front of the barn. If I didn't get this back door open, I wouldn't have any way to escape.

Bang! Bang! Bang! Bang! Time felt like sand running through my fingers.

Bang!

The lock busted and the door flew open. Cool night air flooded inside.

No sign of Belkie or the other guy. I could run now and not get caught.

For a moment, I nearly did. Then I pictured the horrible remains of dead cattle. I remembered how angry and sad I'd been when I saw a magnificent animal like Big Boy so senselessly killed.

I turned back toward the stalls.

First, I'd release Big Boy. Then the others.

I fumbled with the latch on Big Boy's stall. He stomped around inside. The banging of the hammer probably hadn't helped his nerves.

Then once again the overhead lights flooded my eyes and Belkie appeared in the doorway. Standing behind him was Cowle, nightmare big and ugly.

"Do you have a death wish?" Belkie asked. He held a rifle. "This time, fool, I'm armed with bullets. Not tranquilizers."

Big Boy rammed the stall door. The other bulls snorted and roared. The banging and the sudden light had worked up their tempers.

It was act now and die trying, or face certain death later.

I yanked on the stall door.

The set up of the hinges saved my life. When the stall door swung open, it shielded me from the angry bull. It also blocked the path to the back door of the barn behind me.

Big Boy charged out. There was only one direction

for him to go. Toward Belkie, who stood in the open doorway of the work area.

I did not see what happened. I was behind the stall door. I can only imagine how terrible it must have been to face over a thousand pounds of raging bull from only a few feet away.

The ground seemed to shake as Big Boy charged.

Belkie didn't even have time to fire his rifle.

I heard a scream of terror and pain.

Then a second scream.

I peeked around the edge of the stall door.

Belkie was lying on the ground, twisted and huddled.

Past him, in the work area, I caught flashes of Big Boy as he stomped, snorted, and charged, chasing the other man in circles. That's where the second scream had come from. Big Boy was trying to gore Cowle.

I stepped forward and grabbed the rifle that lay on the concrete.

I didn't have to worry about Belkie. He was moaning and twitching, still alive, but in too much agony to bother me.

Big Boy flashed past the doorway again. Cowle screamed more. Big Boy was so angry and wanted the man so bad, he didn't even notice the open door.

I thought of going into the work area to try to rescue the big man. But what would I be able to do? Big Boy takes up a lot of room, and there was no way to stop him when he was angry. Not unless I shot him.

For a moment, I wondered if I should. As valuable as Big Boy was, I couldn't stand by and let a man die. Then, through the doorway, I saw the man scramble to the roof of the pickup truck.

Big Boy lowered his head and charged. The truck rocked and sent Cowle flying. Before Big Boy could get around the truck, the big foreman opened the door and jumped inside.

Big Boy backed up and took another run. More than a thousand angry pounds' worth of run. He hit the passenger door with the great, bulging muscles of his shoulder and kept pushing. The truck tilted and fell on its side.

At that point, I closed the door and sealed off the work area. Big Boy was safe and guarding the truck. Cowle was safe as long as he wasn't stupid enough to try to climb out of the truck. If he couldn't climb, he couldn't escape while I waited for the police.

There was a phone near the light switch. I picked it up and dialed 9-1-1.

"Hello," I said when the operator answered. I gave her the ranch's location and explained the situation.

I looked down at Belkie. His face twisted as he moaned. Blood ran from his nose. His fine clothing was stained with manure from the concrete floor.

I thought of all the animals Belkie had killed and what he had intended to do to me and Stephanie. I thought about the pain Belkie felt, lying on the floor. And I considered asking the operator to tell the ambulance driver he could take his time. But I didn't.

Twenty-Four

Finally, I could think of hockey again. I also remembered my promise to Luke. I didn't understand why he needed help to get through the season, but it was a promise I had made. And promises are made to be kept.

He tested it almost right away.

It was a Friday night home game against the Spokane Chiefs. The Riverside Coliseum was nearly full of fans when we stepped onto the ice for pregame warmups. People in Kamloops really know hockey. They like to watch the players on both teams, scouting for weaknesses and strengths.

Players on both teams skated circles—the Chiefs in their end, we Blazers in ours. If you've ever watched warmups, you know the first part is relaxed. We skate slow, loosening up our muscles. The coach will give us some pucks to pass around. We chat with each other, kick the pucks around, and look into the stands to see if our girlfriends are watching.

I already knew where Stephanie was. Five rows above the penalty box. She had waved at me. I had waved at her. Then I had pretended to be cool, even though inside I was dancing. We already had plans to go to a movie when I got back from the road trip with the Buffalo Sabres.

Life was perfect.

Well, nearly perfect.

I came out from behind the net and saw Luke Zannetti skating toward the Chiefs. It was easy to see why. Luke was chasing one of the pucks that had squirted loose from our half of the ice.

Trouble was, a moose in a Chiefs uniform was skating straight toward Luke. This was a moose disguised as a human being, a moose named Lefty Donning who played defense for the Chiefs. He had a reputation as one of the league's dirtiest players.

Luke's head was down as he skated, and he didn't see it coming. Lefty Donning leveled Luke with a body check*. The impact slammed Luke onto the ice. He slid into the boards. Donning stood above Luke and waited for him to get up.

This wasn't good.

I knew why it had happened. Even though he had been playing badly, Luke was still feared as one of the league's best players. If the Chiefs could knock him off his game with a dirty move, so much the better. Worse stuff has happened. Especially from Lefty Donning.

The ref started to skate toward them.

So did I, but a lot faster. I got there just as Luke got to his feet. Trouble was, I didn't have much backup. The other guys on the team didn't like Luke much and were taking their time.

"Hey, baby," Lefty said to Luke. "Want to cry or want to fight?"

I stepped between them.

"He wasn't even looking, jerk," I said.

"Drop your gloves, pal." He dropped his. He took off his helmet. "Let's do it."

I smiled at Lefty. Five other Chiefs' players stood behind him. But after facing Belkie and his rifle, this was nothing.

"Not this time."

"Chicken?"

"No," I said. "If we fight, you're off the ice with a penalty. It's always easier for our team to beat yours when they let you play. I mean, it's easier to go around you than around a garbage can. And you smell about the same."

He swung his fist toward my head. He didn't know what I knew—that the referee was behind him. The ref managed to grab Lefty's arm. Two linesmen moved in to help.

Luke and I skated away.

"Thanks," he said.

I stared at Luke's face. "Your nose is bleeding," I said.

"Big surprise," he said.

"What's that?"

"Nothing."

We crossed the center line. Luke skated to the bench for a towel to wipe his face. A minute later, he was back on the ice. He caught up to me and tugged on my sleeve.

"Look," he said, skating beside me and speaking in a low voice. "That hit really hurt. Can you cover me during the game?"

"Cover you?"

"Yeah," he said. "I'm not going to try to fool you. A couple times up and down the ice, and I'll be close to dead. My legs are gone and I can hardly breathe. I need you to cover me."

"But—"

"I won't skate into their end as deep. I won't come back to our net as far. I'm going to float around the middle as much as I can. That should get me through the game."

"Luke, if you're hurt, tell Coach Price. He—"

Luke pulled on my sleeve again. We were skating almost visor to visor.

"There's one person in the league who's smart enough, strong enough, and fast enough to carry our line with a center who can't skate. You. I'm begging you man, just get me through this."

I shook off his grip. He was asking me to do something that wasn't good for the team. I thought again of drugs and wondered if he was into something bad.

"Luke, whatever it is, you need to get help."

He spun me so that I had to look into his face. Behind his visor, I could see traces of dried blood around his nose. His eyes were filled with tears.

"I *am* getting help," he said. "You're the only one who knows. Just get me through the season. In the summer, I'll get better."

I started to say no. He saw it coming.

"I saved your life, man. I didn't want to throw that at you. But I saved your life."

"Fine," I said. I was half mad at the situation, half mad at him. "I'll do it. One condition, though. We do it my way."

Twenty-Five

My way was simple. If Luke wanted the line to play for him, he'd have to play for the line. I told him if he hung on to the puck for more than three seconds, the deal was off.

Our line started one minute and thirty-two seconds into the game. Still 0–0. The faceoff* was just over our blue line, on the left side. Luke played at center. Gordie Penn played at right wing. I was along the boards at left wing.

The ref dropped the puck. Luke picked it clean in midair, slapping it waist high toward me. I knocked it down with my glove. The Chiefs' forward slammed me, but I spun away, digging for the puck with one hand on my stick.

Gordie cut toward the middle. I flicked it ahead to him.

Luke skated hard right, covering Gordie's position.

Gordie made a move on their center, then backhanded a pass over to Luke.

I was busting up the ice. Luke saw me, and as the puck touched his stick, he fired it back toward me.

Perfect pass. I took the puck in just over their blue line, then faded toward the boards, drawing their defenseman. As the defenseman made his move and opened a gap between his skates, I shoveled the puck toward Gordie, who still covered center ice.

Gordie batted it to Luke, who was already around the other defenseman. Luke was alone on the goalie, cutting in from the far side. All he needed to do was pick up some speed, and he could cut back to center.

It wasn't happening. Luke was half bent, obviously in pain. He found the strength to straighten. He brought his stick back to fire a slap shot.

The goalie set himself. Because of Luke's position, all the goalie had to do was stand still. No way could Luke score.

Luke continued the smooth flow of his shot. Somehow, just before impact, he snapped his wrist at a near impossible angle and flicked the puck toward Gordie.

Gordie?

He was waiting directly in front of the net. The goalie had moved so far to the side that all Gordie had to do was keep his stick on the ice and redirect the puck into the wide-open net.

The red light behind the net flashed.

We'd scored.

I looked over at Luke to see if he had enjoyed the bang-bang-bang passing display.

But Luke was on the ice. Curled into a ball.

From as far away as I was, I could see the blood running out from under his helmet onto the ice.

Twenty-Six

I wore a cowboy hat as I stepped into the hospital room. Luke was in a bed on the far side, sitting up with his back against pillows. The window blinds were open, and afternoon sunshine threw lines of shadow across his face and across the top of his bald head.

"Hey, Cowboy," he said. "Ever notice how loud your boots are? I heard you down the hallway a mile away."

"Nice pajamas," I said. "Green is definitely your color."

"Thanks," he said. "It's a real pain, trying to keep the fashion photographers out of my room."

I pulled up a chair and sat beside his bed. I didn't, however, take off my cowboy hat. That could wait until the rest of the guys showed up.

"Heard you did good in California," he said.

"Not bad," I answered. "But let me tell you, the NHL is a whole new game. Those guys are big, fast, and smart."

"You scored a goal."

"Yup." I grinned. I dug into my pocket. "In fact, here it is. The guys saved it for me."

My first National Hockey League goal! There had been a scramble in front of the San Jose Sharks' net. The puck had popped loose in my direction. Without thinking—because there wasn't time—I'd fired high, catching the top shelf of the net. It had been such a shock, I didn't remember to ask the referee for the puck. One of the Sabres had done that for me and had brought it over with a grin on his face as big as the one on mine.

Luke held the puck. I watched his face. There wasn't much color in it. There were dark circles beneath his eyes. Pain had left its mark. But there was a smile in his eyes as he handed the puck back.

"Good job, Cowboy. I mean that."

"I know you do," I said. I flipped him the puck. "I want you to have it."

His eyes widened. "It's your first NHL goal. I can't take it."

"Luke. Here's the deal. When you get your first NHL goal, you send me your puck. We'll be even."

"Sure," he said, his voice so soft I could barely hear it.

"I mean it," I said. "From what I heard, you might be back on the ice by next season."

"And I might not be," he said. "How much do you know?"

"Leukemia," I said. "You've got early symptoms of it. Not fun."

Leukemia. It was a form of cancer where the body produced too many white blood cells. It could cause bleeding and shortness of breath. Just like Luke's nosebleeds and problems on the ice.

"They're getting it early," he said. "My chemotherapy starts soon."

Luke grinned and rubbed his bald head. "I knew the treatments would make my hair fall out. So I shaved my head. That way no one would know about the leukemia."

"Stephanie helped me figure that out," I said. "Your Michael Jordan story was pretty lame."

This was my first chance to speak to Luke. The morning after the game against the Chiefs, I'd flown to California for my games in the NHL. "How long have you known you have it?"

"Not long," he said. "I started to get those nose bleeds all the time. It was strange, so I went to a doctor. One in Vancouver, just in case something was seriously wrong. I didn't want anyone to know. Not even my parents. I just wanted to get through the season. I was hoping the chemo would help, and after the summer I'd be ready to play again. I was afraid if anyone knew, the Montreal Canadians would find out and I'd never have a chance."

Luke stared at the puck in his hands. "I'm sorry, Josh. I shouldn't have taken things out on you."

"Don't sweat it," I said.

Luke opened his mouth to say something. Then he shut it and went back to staring at the puck.

"What?" I said.

"All right." He took a breath. "I might die, you know. I mean, they say with this form of leukemia, I've got a great chance of beating it. But there's still the chance I won't."

"I'll be praying for you," I said.

"I know," he said. "That's what I want to ask you about. You go to church and know about God. I mean, the possibility of dying is scary . . ."

I think I knew what he meant.

"Luke, I'm not going to paint you some picture where the world is perfect if you believe in God. All I can tell you is what my dad once said."

I closed my eyes to concentrate. When I opened them again, I said, "We all know that we've got a body and brain. What's invisible is the third part. Our soul. If you can believe in love, something just as invisible, you can understand having a soul."

This wasn't something guys talked about much, and I didn't know if I should continue, but he was listening hard. So I said, "And if the soul is something that truly exists, then later, when your body is gone, your soul lives on. Dad tells me to think of my time on earth as the beginning of a journey that will go on forever."

Luke was nodding. We might have spoken about it more, but footsteps reached us from the hallway. A whole herd of footsteps. It was the other guys from the team.

They crowded into Luke's room wearing various kinds of hats.

I stood. If Luke had more questions, we'd talk later. For now, though, there was something we had to do.

I took off my cowboy hat and rubbed my head.

Luke's jaw dropped in surprise.

One by one the rest of the guys took off their hats. Some were grinning. Some were serious. All of them stared at Luke.

Luke stared right back at twenty-one bald heads.

"Need sunglasses, Luke?" someone asked.

"I don't get it," he said.

"We're a team," I told him. I rubbed my hairless head again, almost to convince myself I was bald. The smooth skin of my skull sure felt weird. "When you start growing your hair back, so will we."

Lightning on Ice Series

Rebel Glory

B. T. McPhee, the star defenseman of the Red Deer Rebels, likes his chances of making it as a pro. But he doesn't like the small "accidents" that may keep his team from making the playoffs—and keep him off the team. In the spotlight of high-pressure hockey, B. T. has no choice. Unless he can unravel the mystery, the team's season—and his own career—will surely end. (ISBN 0-8499-3637-3)

All-Star Pride

Hog Burnell is playing on a WHL All-Star Team touring Russia. The goal is to beat the Russian All-Stars in the best-of-seven series to be shown as a television special. Hog could use the money that will come with a series win by the WHL All-Stars. But it doesn't take Hog long to discover there's plenty more money to be made along the way . . . if he's willing to pay the price for it. (ISBN 0-8499-3638-1)

Thunderbird Spirit

Dakota Smith plays for the Seattle Thunderbirds. He's fast and smooth with a shot as deadly as most pros. Unfortunately, there are more than a few unwilling to accept a Native American in hockey. For Mike "Crazy" Keats, haunted by a troubled background that fast makes him friends with Dakota, it means hockey just got more complicated. Racial hatred takes Mike and Dakota into a web of violence and deceit that makes winning this year's championship the least of their concerns.
(ISBN 0-8499-3639-X)

Winter Hawk Star

Riley Judd is a star center for the Portland Winter Hawks. His great playing skills are exceeded only by his oversized ego, which gets in his way. Given the choice of working with street kids in roller hockey or getting kicked off the team, Judd takes what he thinks is the easy way out. Along with a teammate named Tyler Watson, he discovers that it could cost their lives to give the kids the help they really need.
(ISBN 0-8499-3640-3)

Blazer Drive

When Josh Ellroy, left-winger for the Kamloops Blazers, and his dad find more than a dozen dead cattle on the family ranch, Josh has some serious decisions to make. On one hand Western Hockey League playoffs are ahead, plus a chance to play in the Naional Hockey League. On the other hand, there's a beautiful and interesting girl who believes more prize bulls will be killed. Josh is afraid of what will happen if he gets involved. As he learns more, he's afraid of what will happen if he doesn't. (ISBN 0-8499-3983-6)

Chief Honor

They said it wouldn't happen—but it did. A woman goalie! A messy lawsuit makes the Spokane Chiefs the first WHL team with a female player. And for Jewels Larken, Chiefs goaltender, the rest of a season in the publicity shadow of teammate goaltender Lauren Cross promises to be the ultimate nightmare. Hiding behind a carefully built wall of hatred and scorn, Jewels is almost glad for the steroids scandal which will ruin Lauren's career. Until he discovers that someone's trying to frame him too. And worse, he's learning that Lauren's as easy to like as she is impossible to trust. (ISBN 0-8499-3984-4; available 3/97)

Western Hockey League

The Western Hockey League
Encourages You to Stay in School

The players of the Western Hockey League are working hard toward reaching the dream of playing in the National Hockey League.

That's not the only thing they are working hard at. They know that as hard as they work on the ice, it is important to work just as hard in the classroom. Education makes them better players and better people.

The Western Hockey League makes sure that all of its players have the opportunity to succeed all the way through high school and into college or university. Players work together with their teachers, counselors, and teams to learn both on and off the ice.

WHL players know when the going gets tough, on or off the ice, you must never give up. A good education will help you make better decisions about what to do with the puck, or what to do in life situations.

Whenever you have a question or a problem in school, ask your teacher or your counselor for help. And no matter what, STAY IN SCHOOL.